# STEP FATHER CHRISTMAS

## L. D. LAPINSKI

Orion

This story is for Lena,
because she asked
to hear it

ORION CHILDREN'S BOOKS

First published in Great Britain in 2023
by Hodder & Stoughton

10 9 8 7 6 5 4 3 2 1

Text copyright © L. D. Lapinski, 2023
Cover illustration © Nicolas Rix, 2023

A CIP catalogue record for this book
is available from the British Library.

ISBN 978 1 510 11269 8
Exclusive ISBN 978 1 510 11293 3

Typeset in Baskerville by Jouve (UK),
Milton Keynes

Printed and bound in Great Britain by
Clays Ltd, Elcograf S.p.A.

The paper and board used in this book
are made from wood from responsible
sources.

Orion Children's Books
An imprint of Hachette Children's Group
Part of Hodder & Stoughton Limited
Carmelite House
50 Victoria Embankment
London EC4Y 0DZ

An Hachette UK Company
www.hachette.co.uk
wwww.hachettechildrens.co.uk

Dear Reader,

Firstly, thank you for choosing this book to read. You have excellent taste, if I do say so myself.

Secondly, I must take this opportunity to alert you to the fact that *Stepfather Christmas* has been written in twenty-five truly terrific chapters, which means it can be read in a very special way. No, I don't mean back to front, upside down or underwater. I mean that the most exciting way to enjoy this story is to read it in the style of an advent calendar:

Start on the 1st of December and read one chapter each day during the lead-up to Christmas, getting to the final chapter on Christmas Day itself. It's a book that can be read alone, or with someone special, or in a group all together!

Are you ready for a festive mystery full of family secrets and yuletide fun? Then settle down with a hot chocolate, and let's begin . . .

# One

'There's tinsel in my sandwich.'

Mum looked up from the heap of boxes she was in the middle of. 'Well, that's festive.'

I picked the tinsel out from the peanut butter, wondering if it had any nutritional value. I glanced around the room. There was tinsel *everywhere*, along with miniature reindeer, angels and stars, which were scattered over the living room like snow. We were in the middle of putting the Christmas tree up.

Mum extracted herself from the boxes, one hand on

the sideboard to steady herself, trying not to knock over the photo that took pride of place – me, Mum and my big brother Will on Mum's graduation day a few years ago, when she became Dr Helen Hall: Super-Vet. 'I always forget how much Christmas stuff we have until I get it all down from the loft,' she said once she was finally free.

'I think it multiplies up there,' I said. 'I don't remember half of this.'

'I know! Who made this?' She held up an MDF-and-PVA-glue Nativity scene where Mary and Joseph both looked like Shrek. 'Was it Will?'

'No way,' Will answered for me, slouching into the living room, his PuzzoCube glued into his hand as usual. 'I don't draw people like that.' He sat down and began solving the cube without looking up.

'Well, it wasn't me,' I said.

Mum shrugged. 'Maybe it was one of your cousins . . .' She began searching through another bag.

Will pulled a face at me that said *Every year, right?* And I nodded back at him.

Every year, Mum goes as full-on for Christmas as her budget will allow. That's not particularly far, but she always manages to transform the living room into a grotto, complete with hundreds of fairy lights, a massive Christmas tree and so many pillows and rugs you struggle to know where to sit down. When we were little, it was like magic. Now I'm ten, and Will's thirteen, it feels like we've both outgrown it a little – but even though the magic has faded, I haven't said anything to Mum because she loves it so much, and it's always a special family time for the three of us. Mum started going all-out on Christmas back when it was just her and Will, and when I came along it was only a few months before she was dressing me as a baby reindeer for the family photos.

Will twisted his PuzzoCube in his hands.

'Are you winning?' I asked. I was longing to get back

to my own hobby: reading through the latest *Murder at the Tea-Party* storybook I'd got from the library. The main characters are these schoolgirls who run a secret detective agency, and the stories always have these amazing plot twists.

'I'm sort of winning,' Will said, clicking something into place. 'I'm third in the Collectors' League.'

I had no idea what that meant. Will's cube was from the 1970s, a sort of less-successful version of the more famous puzzle cube, where the goal wasn't to get all the colours on the same side, but to copy patterns on collectable cards. He'd picked it up at a jumble sale a few months ago and it had quickly become his obsession.

'Cool,' I said.

'Oh, actually . . .' Mum's head popped up like a jack-in-the-box. 'I'm glad you're in the same room, you two. I wanted to tell you something.' And she suddenly went bright red, like the painted noses on the plastic reindeer.

4

'What's up?' Will lowered his cube. 'Is it bad?'

'No, no, it's nothing bad,' Mum said, going impossibly redder. 'It's a nice thing.'

'Tell us,' I said. 'Come on, or we'll start guessing.'

Will started guessing anyway. 'Are we being sent to boarding school? Are we getting a dog?'

'No! Sorry, no.' Mum sighed, and brushed some of the dust off her jumper. 'Well . . . Harper, Will . . . we're going to have a guest. For the Christmas season.'

'But we always have Christmas with just the three of us,' I cried.

Will narrowed his eyes. 'Who? What guest?'

'His name's Nick,' Mum said. 'We actually met at Farmer Llama's petting zoo last year, and stayed in touch. He's nice.' She was still as red as a tomato.

'But who *is* he?' I asked. 'Is he working with you?'

'No, he's . . .' Mum twisted an old stocking, then sighed in resignation. 'He's my boyfriend. OK, happy now?'

5

Me and Will groaned in perfect unison.

Mum doesn't have many boyfriends – she doesn't have time, for starters. Because she's a vet, she's always zooming out the house to go and see to people's sick dogs or cats or stick insects. The last boyfriend who Will and I met, Disaster Dave, used to build cathedrals out of spent matches, and even now we still find empty matchboxes stuffed into the backs of drawers and used as bookmarks. But we hadn't met one of her boyfriends for a long time. Years, actually. The thought of Mum seeing someone seriously was . . . *weird*.

'What's he like?' I asked, as Will went back to his puzzle.

Mum beamed in response. 'Oh, he's ever so nice. A real gent. He loves animals, and works seasonally up at Farmer Llama's.'

'Oh.' As stories went, it wasn't exactly thrilling. 'When's he coming?'

'He'll be round this afternoon for a cup of tea' – Mum checked her watch – 'and to meet you and Will, of course. And as long as we all get on, he'll be staying here for a few weeks.'

I wasn't sure I liked the idea of there being a stranger in the house, but if Mum liked him enough to keep in touch for a whole year, he must be nice. I nodded. 'OK then.'

Mum's smile softened a bit. 'Thanks for being understanding, Harper. He won't be under your feet. He leaves very early and often comes home very late, because of the animals. But you're being really kind – I know it's not cool to think about your mum having a boyfriend.'

Will muttered something under his breath, but Mum either didn't hear or pretended not to.

We carried on wrestling with putting the tree up, Will peeling himself away from his PuzzoCube long enough to put the star on top as he was the tallest. We'd just tidied some of the boxes away and were in the kitchen putting the kettle on when the doorbell rang.

Mum went white, then red, then white again like a malfunctioning candy cane. 'Oh, he's early!'

'Tell him to wait,' Will said, stuffing bags-for-life into the cupboard under the stairs.

'I can't do that, Will, don't be silly. Just clear some space on the sofa for him to sit. Harper, will you sort out the teapot?' She bustled off to the door, tinsel trailing from where it was stuck to one of her sleeves.

Will looked at me, shaking his head. 'She must really like him.'

'I hope he's normal,' I said, pouring the boiling water. 'Not another one with a weird hobby.'

The front door opened, and I heard laughter and a man's voice. Will scuttled away into the living room and I put the lid on the teapot just as Mum came into the kitchen.

'. . . and this is Harper,' she said, happily.

I put on my brightest smile and turned to say hello. Except the word never made it out of my mouth.

'Hello there, Harper,' Nick said in a quiet but friendly way. But although my mouth was open, I still couldn't speak because I was too stunned.

The man in front of me . . . my mum's new boyfriend . . . he had grey-white hair, a white beard, a comfy round stomach and was wearing red trousers and big black boots . . .

'Merry Christmas,' he said with a smile.

# TWO

Alright, there was no need to overreact. It was probably just a coincidence that my mum's new boyfriend looked *exactly* like Father Christmas.

Will came in from the living room and said hello without much enthusiasm, apparently not noticing or caring that this man who had suddenly walked into our lives looked like he had stepped off a Christmas card and was even giving a little *ho ho ho* chuckle as he talked. Now he'd come in and taken his boots off, I could see he was wearing socks with Christmas puddings on them. And he was a big man – fat, but in the way a strongman was fat – broad at the shoulders and looking like he could bench-press a car.

'How's that tea coming on, Harps?' Mum nudged me.

I stopped staring and began making the tea like a robot. There was no way I was the only one who had noticed. Will was probably staying quiet for now, but thinking of something funny to whisper to me as soon as he got me alone. Typical Mum, picking someone else we'd be laughing at in a few months . . .

'Oh, no tea for me, thanks,' Nick said.

'Can we get you something else?' Mum asked.

'A glass of milk, if it's not too much trouble?'

I nearly fell head-first into the fridge. Was he doing this on purpose?

'Oh, we only have oat milk,' Mum said. 'Is that alright?'

'Wonderful. Perhaps a little cinnamon in it, to give it some Christmas spice?'

I kept waiting for someone to state the obvious. I couldn't believe no one else was commenting on this. I searched for the cinnamon while Nick asked Will about his puzzle cube and Mum put Christmas cookies on a plate. Everyone was ignoring the Santa-shaped elephant in the room!

When Mum and Nick went through into the living room, Will stayed behind to help me with the tray.

'Well?' I whispered. 'What's that about?'

Will blinked at me. 'What's what about?'

'Him!' I nodded at the doorway. 'He looks just like . . .'

'Like what?' Will was impatient.

'Like Santa!' I whispered.

Will snorted. 'Very funny.'

'I'm not joking! Come on, he looks *exactly* like Santa. You have to admit it.'

Will looked at me like I was three snowflakes short of a blizzard. 'He's wearing his red work clothes, and he's got whiteish hair. But he's just a normal man, Harper.'

13

'You just like him because he asked about your cube.'

'I don't.' Will picked up the tray and carried it through whilst I followed with the cookies.

Mum had turned on the tree lights and the living room looked wonderful and festive, even with the boxes not yet put away. The plastic reindeer in the window were lit up too, casting gold sparkles over the fake snow. The place felt cosy and special . . . and that wasn't just because Santa's double was in the room. If anything, it felt weird there being a fourth person in the house.

Nick was admiring Mum's collection of little porcelain snow babies. He had his blue and red tartan sleeves rolled up to the elbow, and I could see he had tattoos on his forearms, but I couldn't make out what they were.

'Thank you,' Mum said as Will put down the tray. 'It's lovely to have everyone together in one room finally.'

*Finally?* Will and I shot each other a look. Even if Nick and Mum had been chatting for a solid year, we'd

14

only heard about him this morning. I passed the cookies round, not trusting myself to speak as Nick took one to go with his glass of milk. His grey-white hair was longer than I'd first noticed, tied back in a bun at the base of his head.

'So, you work at the petting zoo?' Will asked him, as if Nick was auditioning for the role of Mum's Boyfriend, and Will was testing out his suitability.

Nick smiled. 'That's right. I've worked there on and off for a few years, seasonally. They only get me in for the winter months.'

'How come?' I asked.

'Because they don't keep the animals I look after on the farm all year round. Most of the year they're up in Finland, grazing the landscape.'

'What animals do you look after?' Will frowned.

'Reindeer.'

I dropped my Christmas cookie into my tea. It floated

for a moment, and then sank. No one else seemed to have noticed.

'Reindeer? Oh, so they bring them over for Christmas?' Will asked.

'Yes, they dress them up with bells and take them into schools and so on,' Mum said. 'They always have a vet come in to make sure they all have a clean bill of health beforehand. That's how Nick and I met last year. It makes for an interesting change of pace for me – usually it's all pigs and goats at the farm.'

I coughed to try and activate my voice. 'And between the school visits and whatever, you look after them, Nick? The reindeer?'

'Oh yes,' he beamed. 'They're marvellous animals, they really are. Intelligent, hardy, don't scare easily like horses . . . I've always worked with them.' He sipped at his glass of oat milk, and that's when I noticed his tattoos were reindeer – a skull, complete with antlers, on his left arm and a nice living reindeer surrounded by flowers on his right. With his red uniform, black braces, big belt and white hair, he fit into our Christmassy lounge perfectly, as if Santa himself really had dropped by for a glass of milk. How was no one else saying anything about it?

After we'd all watched a classic episode of *The Muppet Show*, Nick said it had been nice to meet us, and he'd be bringing his suitcase over the next day. I managed to stay polite and not stare as Nick pulled his big boots back on and zipped up a (thankfully blue) coat. When Mum shut the door behind him, she only gave a small sigh of relief.

'Well, what do you think?' she asked with a worried smile.

Will shrugged. 'He's alright,' he said, picking up his puzzle. 'I guess.'

Mum smiled properly. 'What about you, Harper?'

I tried to arrange my thoughts. 'He's . . . he's like Santa,' I said,

17

Mum blinked, then laughed. 'Oh, you mean with the red suit and the reindeer? Poor guy. Farmer Llama's makes him wear that – they say it looks more Christmassy. But did you like him?'

'I think so,' I said. 'It was just hard to see past the Santa stuff.'

'Well, he won't be dressed like that forever. Just don't mention it in front of him. I think it makes him feel a bit embarrassed,' she said firmly. 'Now – mince pies, anyone? We need to start doing our annual taste-test.'

'I volunteer,' Will said, leaping to his feet.

# Three

Everyone in our house usually sleeps late on a Saturday, but that weekend I was woken up early by my nose tingling. In a good way.

I rolled over and tried to figure out what was happening, until my brain kicked in and told my nose that the tingle was caused by the scent of something delicious. Now that was suspicious. Nothing tasty ever happened in our house before noon. I woke myself up properly, wondering why Mum was cooking first thing in the morning. Maybe she'd taken Christmas too far and finally lost her marbles. Either way, I wanted to find out.

Wrapped in my old dressing gown and slippers, I tiptoed downstairs. I could hear Mum's tablet playing some music in the kitchen, so let myself in to ask what was cooking. But Mum wasn't alone.

Nick was there. Already.

They were sitting at the table together, in front of the tablet, the two of them welling up with tears as they watched a department store advert. The advert showed a tiny starfish who longed to be on top of the seaweed Christmas tree, but wasn't big enough to be noticed.

'Are you two alright?' I asked.

Mum jumped. 'Oh, Harper. Did we wake you up?'

'I smelled something,' I said, looking around for the potentially-delicious culprit. 'Are you cooking?' On the tablet screen, the tiny starfish had been spotted by a school of fish, who were admiring it.

'That would be me,' Nick said, smiling. His grey-white hair was tied back in a plait today, and his red work clothes swapped for blue jeans and a plaid shirt. He didn't look quite like Santa any more, but he also didn't *not* look like Santa, if you know what I mean.

'I'm putting your mum's oven to good use – the first batch should be cool by now.' He left the tablet, where the tiny starfish had at last been placed at the top of the seaweed tree and was lighting up the ocean in a festive display that reminded viewers to do all their shopping at the Swan Brewis department store. Mum clicked her tongue as an email pinged up on her screen saying 'Emergency'.

Meanwhile, Nick picked a wire cooling rack from the counter and held it out to me. It was covered in little gingerbread people, none of them iced yet but all of them smelling absolutely wonderful. 'Take one!'

I did, picking one which had a crumpled head because

I felt sorry for it. 'Thanks. Did you really make all these this morning?'

'Certainly did. There's apple and cinnamon soft cookies in the oven now, and dough ready to become chocolate coconuts waiting in the fridge too. We can make those when I'm back from work later tonight if you like,' he suggested hopefully.

I bit the gingerbread person's leg off to avoid having to decide whether I wanted to bake biscuits with Nick or not. 'This is amazing. We normally just buy our Christmas cookies.'

'We bake sometimes!' Mum objected from where she was examining an X-ray of a dog who'd swallowed a smartphone.

'Yeah, like once a year, and then we eat them all the same afternoon. This is like living in a bakery.' The biscuit was delicious. Warm and spicy and soft and with just enough crunch. Perfect.

'This dog is getting five texts an hour,' Mum muttered. 'He keeps vibrating.'

'Have you got to go in to work?' I asked.

'Probably . . .' she squinted at the X-ray. 'You'll have to come in with me.'

'Oh, what?' I moaned. 'On a Saturday? Can't we just stay at home?'

'On your own? No way! I know what you're both like. You'll have the house burnt down by the time I'm back.'

Nick looked from her to me and back again. 'Why don't they come down to Farmer Llama's?'

We blinked at him in unison.

'I'll be working,' he shrugged, 'but there's plenty of things to do at the farm park to keep them busy, and lots of adults about. I can get them tickets.'

Mum looked a bit unsure. 'I suppose I could drop you both off at the farm park and pick you up after I've sorted Mrs Burzynska's dog .'

'Sounds OK to me,' I said, deciding that at least if we were at the farm park it was better than sitting in the waiting room at the vet's for hours. 'We'll be fine.'

Nick stood up and went to the oven to take out the next batch of cookies, which looked perfectly baked . . . though I noticed he hadn't set any sort of timer. 'That's sorted, then. I'll tell my manager to expect you, and if it starts to rain, or snow, you can hide in the reindeer barn.' He carefully set the cookies to cool on the rack alongside the first batch, drained his hot chocolate mug, put it in the sink, and gave Mum a kiss on the cheek before letting himself out the back door.

Mum had gone red.

I stared around the kitchen, at the heaps of biscuits and the wrapping paper and the cocoa. 'Mum,' I said, trying not to sound too serious, 'you know Nick . . .'

'You don't have to bake with him tonight if you don't want to,' she said quickly. 'You've only just met him, it's fine.'

'No, it's not that. It's . . .' I tried to find the right words. 'He's nice and everything . . . but isn't it a little weird that he acts so much like Santa?'

Mum stared at me. 'Santa?' she repeated.

My cheeks started to go prickly. 'You know, with the hair and the beard and the reindeer and the milk and cookies . . .'

She laughed, then stopped as she saw I was being serious. 'Oh, Harper Hall, come on . . .'

'It's weird!' I insisted.

'You're being really silly,' she sighed. 'And a bit mean. Nick can't help the way he looks and it's not just Santa who likes cookies. You don't have to tease. If you don't like him . . .'

'Mum, I'm not teasing! You don't think there's something a bit odd about him?' I asked. 'Think about it! I mean, what if he really is—'

'Harper, please. He's just a man! He has a normal job

25

working with animals, just like me! I think he's lovely but he isn't magical.' She tutted. 'More's the pity. Stop being so daft, will you?'

I folded my arms as she picked up her tablet and went to the living room to finish her coffee.

Will appeared in the doorway a moment later. 'Do I smell gingerbread?' he asked, sleepily.

'Yeah, Santa delivered it,' I said, passing him the plate.

# Four

Farmer Llama's Petting Zoo and Garden Centre had been at the end of the village, not too far from our house, since the olden days. They had the usual things you'd expect like goats and cows and guinea pigs, but over the past few years they'd been expanding to get some new animals in like alpacas, wallabies and, during the Christmas season, reindeer.

Mum pulled into the car park. The staff had sprayed fake snow all over in an attempt at festivity, but it had been turned a strange shade of yellow by the muddy ground.

'It looks like someone's sneezed,' Will observed as we pulled our wellies on.

Nick was waiting for us by the check-in barn, with wristbands in his hand. He was wearing his red uniform again, with a dark grey beanie hat and shiny black boots. 'VIP access,' he said, proudly brandishing the wristbands. 'These will get you in to all the animal feeding demos, the talks, the petting experiences – the lot.'

I was actually pretty impressed, but tried not to show it.

'Oh Nick, you really didn't have to do that,' Mum gushed. 'VIP passes are expensive!'

Will and I shot each other panicked looks, hoping she hadn't just encouraged him to take the wristbands back. Fortunately, he didn't seem worried.

'No problem, what is staff privilege for?' he *ho ho ho*ed. 'Do you know your way around?'

'I do,' Will said, pulling his wristband on, as I nodded too.

Mum gave us both a squeeze. 'Be good! Go stroke an alpaca for me,' she said. 'And call me if you need anything.'

'We'll be fine.' I let go last. 'Go save the dog!'

'It might be too late to save the phone,' she sighed, before waving and getting back into the car.

Nick stood with us as she pulled away. 'Shall I get you through security?' he asked once she was gone. He led us through the staff-only entrance, skipping the queue and going straight into the farm park.

The place was half-heartedly decorated for Christmas. There were wreaths randomly scattered about, along with a few wooden snowmen and a two-dimensional sleigh painted on to a large piece of plywood, but it was mainly the same farm I remembered from all the school trips, except with lots of fairy lights. It wasn't a bad place to visit, exactly, just a bit tired-looking.

'I have to go feed the reindeer,' Nick said, checking

his watch. 'I'll be over past the Wallaby Walk, if you need me.'

'Thanks,' Will said, eager to get away. 'Come on, Harps. See you later, Nick.'

I followed Will across to the small animal barn, where there was a guinea pig city. Our wristbands meant we could avoid the queue and go straight over to a member of staff who was supervising cuddling the piggies. The supervisor was wearing a green bobble hat.

'Ooh, gold passes,' she said when she saw our wristbands. 'Here, have a hold of Wingus and Dingus.' She gave us a guinea pig each. I love guinea pigs; they're like giant furry jellybeans.

Will stroked his pig. 'What do you think about Nick, then?' he said quietly.

I shrugged. 'I'm not convinced yet.'

'About Nick in general, or about him being Santa?' he teased.

I considered seriously, even though I knew he was making fun of me. 'Both, I guess. I don't know . . . It's like, I want to make sure Mum's OK, you know? That she's picked someone she can count on.'

'I get you.' Will sat down, Wingus the guinea pig sitting on his lap like a squeaking mop-head. 'Mum seems to really like him, and they've been together for a whole year already. This guy could end up being our stepfather. I don't know how I feel about that.'

'Bad?' I chanced.

'I don't *think* so. He actually feels like he could be a nice guy. But we've never had a stepdad. Where would he fit?' Will looked around the barn as if searching for a shelf space to put Nick.

'It's weird that we didn't pick him, and yet he's in our house,' I said.

'Yeah.' Will lifted Wingus into the air to look him in the eye. He sighed. 'You know when you're at school and

31

the teacher pairs you with the kid you don't like? And you can't argue about it? It's like that. Sort of. Except I don't dislike Nick. Not yet anyway.' He gently lowered the guinea pig. 'It's just . . . it's always been the three of us in our family.'

'I know.' I gave Dingus' head a little stroke. 'But they might break up, anyway. We shouldn't worry too much yet.'

'True. Want to go see some lizards?'

We managed to see a lot of the farm because of the wristbands Nick had given us. I even got to feed the meerkats, which was fun until one of them tried to climb into my welly-boot.

'Oh no you don't,' the meerkat keeper said as she lifted it back out. 'Sorry about that, kid.'

We traipsed through the farm as the drizzle started to come down, moving from covering to covering until the only place left to see was the signposted Reindeer Ranch.

'Come on.' Will pulled at my sleeve as I tried to shelter under a tinsel-bordered plastic awning. 'Nick said we could keep dry in the barn.'

The thought of Mum having a serious boyfriend was still making me feel funny, and I wasn't sure I wanted to see Nick again so soon. But what choice did I have? The path led down a slope that evened out towards a huge paddock surrounded by high fences. There were several barns, one with an open garage-style door, one open to the paddock field for the reindeer to walk into, and others which looked unused and locked up. There were food stores and wheelbarrows here and there, as if the area was usually used for storage and only opened to the public for the reindeer season.

But Nick had decorated it spectacularly.

The fences had ribbons, lights, holly and evergreen garlands woven between the links. There were fence-posts skilfully painted to look like candy canes, baubles on the trees surrounding the paddock, glitter in the bushes and the sound of Christmas carols floating through the air. They must have been playing from some hidden speakers.

The reindeer were grazing in the paddock, all of them with fuzzy antlers and wearing red leather harnesses with bells on. And amongst them, walking between the animals holding a bucket of feed, was . . . Father Christmas.

The bottom fell out of my stomach.

Until now, I'd just thought Nick was a man who happened to look like Santa and had leaned into it a *bit* too much. But something about Nick, right then, was different. There was no polite stance to his walk, no awkward friendliness. He looked determined and knowledgeable as he scratched one of the reindeer behind the ears and gave another one a treat. He looked taller too, more imposing and less mildly cheerful. There was a seriousness to his movements with the reindeer, and also a bright sparkle in his eyes that hadn't been there before.

Right then, I had the thought . . . what if he really *was* Santa?

'Good girl, Starlet!' we heard him say as one of the deer trotted over, shaking her head so the bells she wore jingled.

Will looked at me. 'OK,' he said, 'I kind of see what you mean, now.'

# Five

We walked over to the paddock. When Nick caught sight of us and waved, something about his demeanour changed – it was like he softened, or shrank, or something. His smile widened, his stance relaxed, and he even seemed younger.

Weird.

'How did you get on?' he called as we got to the fence.

'Awesome,' Will said. 'The wristbands got us in everywhere, thanks for that.'

'Oh, it was nothing . . . *Easy*, girl.' Nick put out a hand to hold a curious reindeer back by the harness. She was bigger than I'd expected, like a woolly horse with antlers and jingling bells strapped firmly over her huge back and sides. Her large head nudged forward, sniffing at me and Will. She seemed very strong, but even though she was straining to reach us on her massive legs, Nick was only holding her harness with one hand. It didn't seem to be much effort for him to restrain her.

'Hello!' Will said, raising a hand to pat the reindeer. Then hesitated. 'Does she bite?'

'Not children,' Nick said, keeping hold of the animal's harness as Will patted her on the fluffy nose. She snuffled into his hand, searching for scratches. Her grey and brown fur was thick and woolly, wiry like a worn-out scrubbing brush. Her dark eyes shone with a deep intelligence, and I wondered if you could have reindeer as pets. I noticed this one had a name tag – *Lightning*.

'Are they all girls?' I asked, starting to count them.

'Yes,' Nick said. 'You can tell because they've still got their antlers. The boys lose theirs in the winter, so if you see a reindeer with antlers at Christmas, it's a girl.'

*So, Santa's reindeer are all girls*, I thought.

Lightning butted my hand, making me jump. She was a bit scary, being so big, but I gave her a little stroke anyway.

'I've got to pack my stuff away,' Nick said, indicating a wheelbarrow and bags of feed in the field. 'Then we'll see what's occurring with your mum?'

'Eight,' I whispered, as Nick walked away.

'What's that?' Will asked.

'There's eight reindeer. Just like in the song.' I tried to remember. 'You remember, the names of all the reindeer. Dasher, Dancer, Prancer and so on.'

'I think the farm probably got eight reindeer for that exact reason,' Will sighed. 'To make people think of the song. Doesn't mean they're *actually* Santa's reindeer.

Besides, I don't remember a reindeer called Lightning being mentioned. Or Starlet.'

This was true. I watched Nick load up his wheelbarrow for a moment, then looked around. The paddock was surrounded by lovely decorations that almost hid the industrial-looking barns and sheds. It would probably look extra-magical in the dark, when the lights were glowing.

'Look at that!' I pulled Will's sleeve and pointed at a small door on the side of one of the sheds. The shed itself was an especially large one with a huge garage-style door you could have driven a bus through, in addition to the people-sized one. The whole thing was painted a jolly red and there was a beautiful Christmas wreath on the small door.

'Look at what? The wreath?' Will asked, sounding unimpressed.

'Not *that*,' I replied. 'Come on.' I pulled him away from Lightning and down the slope towards the shed.

40

Inside the wreath was a bright yellow sign, which said: ACCESS PROHIBITED.

'Look!' I pointed at the sign.

Will gave me a withering look. 'Harper. This is a farm. It's probably a shed full of machinery that's specially designed to slice off arms and legs if you don't know what you're doing.'

'Or, it's Santa's secret storage! For his list and stuff.' I tried the door. Locked.

'You're breaking and entering now, are you?' Will put his hands on his hips. 'You've lost it.'

'I'm just trying to find out . . .' I pushed the door. It was definitely locked. What was Nick trying to keep secret?

'I am this close to telling Mum you've gone potty,' Will said, his thumb and forefinger practically touching. 'Come *on*, Harper. Why are you so suspicious of the guy?'

'*You* said you saw my point when you saw him with the reindeer!' I pointed out.

Will blushed slightly. 'Well, it was just . . . the look of him right at that second. I didn't mean that he could *actually* be—'

There was a cheerful shout from back towards the paddock, so we went around to find Mum there, chatting to Nick. She looked so happy that I suddenly felt awful for being so suspicious of Nick.

'Hey, Mum.' Will jogged over. 'Did you get the phone out of the dog?'

'Of course I did,' she smiled. 'Are you done here? I thought we could all go to the fayre in the village hall. There's going to be treats, games, snacks.'

'Yes please,' I said. 'Are we going now?'

'Yes, we'll go before all the good treats are taken. Are you able to come with us, Nick?'

My heart sank. I'd been hoping to have Mum

to myself. Or at least to only have to share her with Will.

But no one else seemed to have a problem with Nick coming. 'I'll join you in a little while,' he said. 'I can clock off before closing time, and I don't need to be back until the evening to put the girls to bed.'

'The girls? Oh, the reindeer,' Mum laughed. 'We'll meet you there, shall we?'

*

The village hall was pretty large – it usually did weddings at the weekend – but today it was crammed full of stalls (so many that there were even some outside) all selling festive wares. You simply couldn't move for crocheted snowmen, home-made soaps and mountains of knitted scarves. There was a huge vat of mulled wine warming in a corner, and plates of mince pies were being passed about. Hot chocolate was being scooped out of a huge saucepan  The whole place smelled incredible.

Mum gave us both a few pounds to go and spend on the games. Will threw all his away immediately on the tombola, where the top prize was a huge Lego set. He won a bottle of bubble-bath and a squeaky dog toy shaped like a steak.

'Nice prizes,' I said with a smirk, which made him scowl at me. 'You realise that Lego set probably doesn't even have a ticket in the barrel?' I added. 'I bet no one wins it. Come on, I want to play Splat the Rat.'

The rat turned out to be a black sock stuffed with other socks, and the splatter was a broom handle.

'We need to work as a team,' I said. 'You tell me when they drop the rat, and I'll be ready to splat.'

'Uh-huh . . .' Will wasn't listening; he was looking over my head at some boys from his school who were chatting together. I recognised Henry, his best friend, in the group. 'Just give me a second, Harps . . .' He pushed through the crowd to get to them.

'Everything alright, Harper?' Mum appeared at my side, carrying a bag full of crafted gifts. 'Where's Will off to?'

'His friends were over there,' I said vaguely, my attention on the game. 'Can you help me splat the rat?'

'What? Oh, of course . . . though don't tell anyone. I'm not sure a vet should really be helping with something like this.'

My plan was a success. Mum gave me the nod as soon as the rat was released, and I splatted it in one blow. A grumpy lady gave me a selection box as my prize, taking ages to pull it out from under the counter. I turned to find Will and gloat about my win, but he wasn't with his friends any more. He was standing next to Mum, red-faced and looking upset. Mum was talking to him, looking worried, and she touched his hair as he shook his head.

What was going on?

But before I could ask, Nick arrived.

# Six

'Are you OK?' I whispered to Will when I managed to get closer. He was still a bit red in the face.

'I'm fine,' he said in a voice that sounded like he definitely wasn't fine. He glanced over at the group of boys, who all had their backs to him. It looked like they were laughing.

My heart gave a squeeze. Will had always been one of those people who never got bullied and was always first to get picked for teams . . . why were his mates ignoring him?

I wanted to tell him it would be alright, but Nick was standing with us and it felt awkward, like this should just be a family thing. And anyway, Mum was already speaking.

'Are we having a few more goes on the games?' she asked. I was about to point out that we'd spent all our money, but then realised she was trying to cheer Will up, so kept my mouth shut.

Will shrugged. 'I guess.'

'Have you played Splat the Rat yet?' Nick asked.

I held up my selection box. 'Played it and splatted it.'

'Oh, excellent work! How about the Gift Guesser?' Nick pointed to the table on the far side of the room, staffed by grumpy Mr Poltad who runs the Cash & Carry. He wasn't very popular. At harvest festival time, his shop had donated a lot of tinned food to the school, except it all turned out to be sardines in tomato sauce. Tins and tins and tins of it. And the tins *leaked*, they had to have been pretty old. It took weeks to forget the fishy smell.

But the Gift Guesser stall probably wasn't hiding fish of any sort. The prizes were yours if you guessed correctly what was hidden inside the wrapping paper. However, the gifts were always wrapped in strange shapes to trick you (the correct answer was in an envelope taped to the paper). Last year there'd been an iPhone wrapped up to look like a step-ladder. Weirdly, Rita Islam's dad actually guessed that one right.

Will sighed. 'The chances of winning are so small. Why don't we just play the darts game?'

'The pay-off if you do win is greater though,' Nick said. 'Come on, what do you say?'

I thought it would probably be funny to watch Nick fail to guess correctly, so gave Will a nudge. 'Just a quick go?'

'Fine.' He shoved his hands in his pockets. 'But I'm out of money.'

'I'll handle this,' Nick said. He adjusted his braces, and led the way over to the Gift Guessing stall.

Mr Poltad gave a grimace that might have been a smile when we arrived. 'Try your luck,' he sniffed. 'All money to a good cause.' He patted a tin shaped like a Labrador that had 'For Guide Dogs' written on it.

Nick nodded, and handed over a five-pound note before squinting at the wrapped shapes on the table. There was something that looked like a chair, a plain box, a perfect sphere, and a walking-stick-shaped package. The last one was wrapped in stripy paper so it looked like an oversized candy cane.

'You must raise a lot of money for charity every year,' Mum said, puzzling over the shapes.

'Oh yes, all money goes to a good cause,' Mr Poltad repeated with a sly grin, which made me feel uneasy. I glanced at Will, and he pulled a concerned face at me.

Nick started guessing. He guessed a chocolate bar, a book, bubble bath, a hoover and even a toilet seat, but Mr Poltad shook his head every time. Still, Nick didn't seem too concerned when he finished empty-handed, despite the greasy smile on Mr Poltad's face that now stretched from ear to ear.

'It's all for charity, isn't it?' Nick shrugged. 'Shall I fetch us some mulled wine? Or hot Ribena?'

'Something's up,' I hissed to Will, as Nick and Mum went to join the drinks queue. 'Don't you get a bad feeling?'

'Definitely.'

An idea came to me – maybe this would take Will's mind off whatever was bothering him. 'Let's spy on him, like the characters in the *Murder at the Tea-Party* books! We could solve a mystery!'

Will nodded and pulled my sleeve. 'Come down this way – we can see the back of the stall from back there. Let's see what he's really up to.' He slipped behind a mountain of stacked chairs, past a folded ping-pong table and to the back of the big fake

Christmas tree that was plonked close to Poltad's Gift Guessing stall.

'Shh.' Will put a finger to his lips. Then pointed to the stall. Time to watch, and wait.

We didn't have to wait long.

Perhaps inspired by the win of last year, Mr Islam and Rita were coming up to the stall, looking like they felt lucky.

'Having another go, sir?' Mr Poltad grimaced.

'Well, lightning might strike twice,' Mr Islam beamed, putting a note into the guide dog box. 'And it's for charity.'

'All for a good cause,' Mr Poltad nodded.

He'd said that exact phrase before and suddenly it struck me as suspicious! He'd never actually confirmed it was for *charity*, had he? What was his *good cause*, anyway?

Rita and her dad guessed and guessed what was in the packages, but lightning didn't strike twice. They went away empty-handed, but still smiling.

I looked at Will and shrugged. We had no evidence of wrongdoing yet . . . but then Will prodded me, pointing.

We watched in open-mouthed horror as Mr Poltad carefully unscrewed the bottom of the guide dog box and slipped the money out of it, putting it neatly into his own pocket. The supposed good cause was his own bank account!

I was about to leap out from behind the tree and yell 'THIEF!' when Will took my hand.

'What are you doing?' he whispered. 'If we confront him he'll just deny it. And no one's going to believe us over Mr Poltad! We have to tell Mum. She'll know what to do.' He led me back past the furniture and into the main section of the hall, just as Mum and Nick reappeared holding takeaway cups of hot Ribena.

'Everything alright?' Mum asked.

Will quickly told her, in a low voice, what we'd seen

Mr Poltad doing. Her mouth dropped open. Nick looked horrified, and then furious. 'At Christmas time!' he thundered.

'Do we tell someone?' I asked. 'The police?'

Mum shook her head. 'I think it would be his word against yours, lovelies. And he would just say he was keeping the money safe or something. Well . . . we know not to trust him in future.'

Will made a frustrated noise. 'But he needs . . . a comeuppance!'

'You're right, Will,' Nick said. He handed his drink to Mum, and put his shoulders back. 'Leave it to me.' He marched over to the stall.

'Is he going to beat him up?' Will asked with excitement.

'I don't think so,' Mum said uncertainly.

We watched Nick get to the stall, and to my surprise he pulled out another fiver.

'Another go, sir?' Poltad took the money and slid it into the guide dog tin. 'Good luck.'

Nick gave him what I can only describe as a winner's smile as he turned to face the prizes. He raised a finger, and pointed at the candy cane. 'Three tubes of sweet pastilles,' he said firmly.

Poltad's face contorted, and he flipped open the envelope to reveal Nick was correct. 'Well done,' he said sourly.

But Nick wasn't finished. 'A gift card for the cinema multiplex,' he said, pointing at the chair-shaped package. 'Good wrapping, that one. Now, that round one's a teddy – a panda, specifically. And as for the box . . .' He squinted at it.

My heart was hammering, Will's eyes were like dinner plates and Mum looked as though she was trying not to laugh.

'The box contains a PlayStation 5, with two controllers

55

and a copy of . . . *Dracula Death Mansion 2*,' Nick said smoothly. He turned around to glance at us, and saw us all standing there looking like guppy fish at feeding time. 'That's just my guess, anyway,' he added hastily.

Mr Poltad's face screwed up like a furious ball of paper, but as everyone was watching him he had to open all of the sealed envelopes and admit that Nick had guessed every single gift correctly. He started handing the presents over in a silent rage. Nick passed the spherically-wrapped toy panda to Rita, who had watched the entire game with her mouth open. 'Since you didn't win on your turn,' he said kindly.

He picked up the other three gifts and carried them over to us.

Will was looking at Nick in awe. 'How . . . how did you . . . ?'

'I am excellent at guessing what's inside presents,' Nick said, handing him the square box. 'One of those weird skills.' He shrugged. 'Like knowing when it's about to rain. You should share that prize with your sister, I think.'

'Good thing there's two controllers,' I said, as Mum accepted the sweets and cinema voucher. Everyone was looking at us, and I knew exactly why – it must have looked as though Santa Claus himself had just delivered some presents early.

And I was *sure* that's what had happened.

# Seven

We drove home through the dark, as the sun had set around 4 p.m. All around us, people's houses were lit up with fairy lights, plastic snowmen and flashing signs demanding 'Santa Stop Here'.

I sat in the back with Will, who was retelling Nick's success at the Gift Guessing stall like we hadn't all just been there. '. . . and the look on toady Poltad's face!' he hooted, patting the console now sitting on his lap. 'Best day ever. How did you *know*?'

Nick shrugged from the passenger seat. 'I always just have a hunch, where presents are concerned.'

'Can you come again next year?'

Nick and Mum laughed, and I gave a smile. It was weird thinking of Nick still being here next year. Like part of the family. I wasn't sure if I felt that was a good thing or not. But he'd cheered Will up, so that had to mean something . . . right?

We pulled on to the drive and Nick opened the door for Will so he could stagger out with the box. 'Do you need help setting that up?'

'I'm thirteen,' Will scoffed. 'I don't need help when it comes to a games console. Thanks, though. And for winning it.'

'Oh, you're welcome.'

Mum touched me on the shoulder. 'Are you alright, Harper? You're very quiet.'

'Just thinking.'

'Don't think too hard by yourself, little chick,' Mum said as she unlocked the door. 'A problem shared is a problem halved.'

That was true, but how do you say to your mum: *I think your boyfriend might be Santa Claus but you won't believe me if I say it and also I'm worried that you might like him more than just a little bit and what if he stays forever and will you get married and what's going to happen in the future if you end up married to Santa????*

So I just went 'Mmm' and followed her into the house.

\*

Mum made Will and me peel ourselves away from the new games console after two hours, saying we were going to get square eyes.

We went into my bedroom, because Will's was too Teenage Boy and I wasn't allowed in. I didn't mind – I was pretty sure there were new life forms growing in the mugs scattered all over his desk. My room is half covered in bright posters of my favourite K-Pop band, the Rainbow Catz, and half with drawings I've done of the characters from the *Murder at The Tea-Party* books. Will flopped on to my Rainbow Catz bedspread, and tutted at the poster of the singers I'd taped on to the ceiling. His PuzzoCube was back in his hand, having been given a rest during our console marathon.

'What's going to happen, Will?' I asked.

He raised his head. 'What'd you mean?'

'I mean with Mum and . . . Nick.'

'Oh.' He let his head flop back. 'I don't know.' He shrugged. 'Can you believe he won us a console?'

'I believe it, I was there,' I said, annoyed he'd changed the subject. I picked up my tatty old stuffed Totoro and gave him a squeeze.

'It was cool, wasn't it, how he knew what was in all those presents,' Will said.

'*Another* Santa thing,' I said, unable to stop myself.

'Oh, Harper.' Will pushed himself upright. 'Come on. Not this again.'

'It's not just the guessing what was in the presents! What about the way he handled the reindeer? The cookies and the milk . . .'

'I know he looked like Santa when he was at the barn with the reindeer, but I think anyone with a beard and a red coat would have looked a bit like Santa in *that* situation.' Will gave me a withering look. 'I admit it *is* a bit strange getting used to Nick being here during Christmas, but aren't you a bit old for games like this, Harper?'

I stared at him. 'It's not a game!' I said hotly. 'Look, either he's Santa or . . . he wants to be. There are too many clues!'

'Harper,' he said firmly, 'he might be our new stepdad one day. This is serious. Him and Mum are serious. As weird as it is to think of him being here forever, he's a nice guy and Mum likes him.' He sighed. 'Pretending he's

63

Santa isn't going to make him go away.' He stood up. 'Your room gives me a headache. See you later.'

I watched him leave, feeling mixed up and horrible. Will wasn't wrong – I did feel weird about the idea of having a stepdad, but this whole Santa theory wasn't related to that . . . was it?

I suddenly remembered the way Will's friends had treated him at the fayre, and wished I'd thought to ask him about it. Well, it was too late now. If I asked him about it while he was already annoyed with me, he'd just get all defensive and shut down.

\*

'Is there anything you want to talk about, little chick?' Mum asked as she came to kiss me good night. She gave Totoro a kiss as well.

I was tempted to just hide under the covers, but decided to be brave. 'Mum . . . are you going to get married to Nick?'

She burst out laughing. 'You don't mince your words, do you?' She let out a long exhale. 'I don't know the answer to that question, my love.' She stroked my hair. 'I do really like Nick. Something feels . . . different. It's why I really wanted you both to meet him. But you know even if we did get married one day, nothing would change between us three, yeah? You and your brother will always be my number one priorities.'

'I know.' But the squirmy feeling in my tummy didn't go away. The Rainbow Catz were grinning down at me from their posters and I wanted to hide from their big smiles.

'I promise you'll be the first to know if I even think about making such a huge decision,' she said. 'And I'd never say yes without approval from you and Will first. Night, night, Harper.'

'Night,' I said to the duvet.

The house quietened down and the lights outside,

shining through the curtains from other houses, gradually went out. The moon must have been bright, because there was still a cool glow at my window.

It felt cold, and I was happy to be snuggled in bed.

It was very cosy, and I was so sleepy . . .

A noise made me turn over under the covers.

A bright noise, like metal and light. I sat up, listening.

The noise came again. The *jingling* noise.

I leapt out of bed and pulled the curtains apart, looking in the sky expecting to see a dozen reindeer zooming against the moonlight.

But there was nothing. Even the sound had disappeared.

I sighed and felt silly. Of course. Just my imagination.

I went to pull the curtains closed again, and just before I did I saw a single snowflake drift past the window . . .

# Eight

'Harper! HARPER! WAKE UP!'

I'd been having a very strange dream about unwrapping a Christmas present that never seemed to run out of wrap. Mountains of paper kept peeling off it but I never found what was inside. Weird.

'Harper!' Will ruffled my hair and poked at my duvet. 'Wake up, you've got to see it!'

'Wha–?' I peeled my head off the pillow.

'Wake up and look at the SNOW!' Will threw my

curtains open. A bright white light streamed in, and I sat bolt upright.

'Snow?' I ran to the window to look out at the back garden.

Will was right. Snow covered the grass, the greenhouse, the little plastic slide left on the patio from when we were little. It was good snow, too, the solid kind you can build with, and was piled up deep enough to hide the empty plant pots we had waiting for springtime.

'Let's go out!' Will made to run back to his room for his winter gear.

But I was frowning. 'Will . . .'

'What is it?'

'. . . why hasn't it snowed anywhere else?'

'Huh?' Will came back to the window.

Whilst there was snow covering our back garden, there was no snow *at all* next door. There was none on the tops of the fences, either, or on the road in the distance.

In fact, it looked as though the only place it had snowed last night was over our house.

'Must have been a weird sort of cloud-burst,' Will said, sounding unconvinced.

'Or it's a natural side-effect of having Santa in the house,' I said, perfectly reasonably.

But Will groaned. 'Oh, give it a rest, Harper.'

Mum came in, knocking on the door as she opened it. 'Have you seen? Isn't it magical!'

'It's only in our garden,' I pointed out.

'Mostly, yes . . . a very interesting meteorological phenomenon,' Mum said, coming to look out the window. 'There must have been a temperature change, or maybe an aeroplane flying overhead caused a microclimate disturbance in the cloud layer.'

'OR,' I started, but Will glared at me, so I shut my mouth again but not before sticking my tongue out at him.

Mum didn't seem to have noticed. 'It's a good thing it's Sunday. If you want to go outside, you can. I'll make you some porridge to warm you up.'

*

Outside was just plain bizarre. Alright, it wasn't as if there was *no* snow anywhere but our garden – there were a few piles and bits of slush around the houses either side, and a sprinkling on the neighbouring rooftops – but there was nowhere near as much anywhere else as there was around our house.

I stood out on the patio, the snow over the feet of my red wellies, just looking at the perfect white blanket covering everything. The sunlight was making the heaps and drifts twinkle, and the air was crisp and cold. The garden looked like it had been painted, the best Christmas card ever.

'CANNONBALL!' Will yelled, running past me and jumping bum-first into the deepest snowdrift near the shed. He went in up to his waist. 'Oh.'

'Help me build a snowman,' I said, starting to pile snow together on the patio.

Will dragged himself free and fished the sweeping brush from where it had been propped up against the shed. He swept the roof of the shed clear of snow before letting himself inside and coming out with the buckets and spades we used to take to the beach. 'Here.' He handed me one set. 'Let's do a proper job, like in *The Snowman* film.'

We started scooping snow into the buckets, and had a good pile by the time Mum called us in for porridge and orange juice. I was a bit worried the whole garden would melt away to nothing if we lingered, so bolted my breakfast down in two minutes flat. Will was right behind me, and thankfully the snow was still there when we ran outside again.

It took ages, and we used snow from every bit of the garden  The fluff from on top of the frozen pond, the

71

swept-up frozen stuff from the patio slabs, and the proper snow from the grass. Will even collected snow from the tops of the bird feeders and the branches of the old cherry tree.

The snowman wasn't quite like the one from the film, but it wasn't too far off. It had a good shape, and defined arms and legs, and a smiley head that Will spent ages on, running his finger along the smile until it was a frozen line deep in the ice. We didn't have a tangerine for the nose, so we had to pick some of the smooth stones from around the pond for that and his eyes, but he looked very pleased with the result.

'He needs a hat and scarf!' Nick came up behind us, carrying a tray as we admired our handiwork. On the tray were two steaming mugs of hot chocolate with squirty cream and marshmallows. I wondered when he'd got back from his morning shift with the reindeer.

'Thanks, Nick.' Will handed me one and took the other for himself.

I hadn't realised how cold my fingers were until that moment, and the cup was wonderfully warm. 'These are fancy!' There was a tiny miniature gingerbread man nestled in the cream, reminding me of Will, waist-deep in the snow.

'I'm famous for my hot chocolates,' Nick laughed, a soft *ho ho ho*. 'But what about your poor snowman? Isn't he underdressed?'

'We don't have a lot of spare stuff,' Will shrugged. 'I think last time we had snow, we dressed him as a vet using Mum's old uniform.'

Nick gave his white beard a stroke. 'Let me see what I have . . .' and he wandered back into the house with the tray.

I sipped my hot chocolate. It was incredible. It tasted just like a melted chocolate bar in a mug. I looked at Will. 'If he comes out with a red hat, I'm just going to ask him.'

But he didn't. Nick returned with a tweed flat cap and a grey wool scarf that looked as though they'd seen better days. They were ideal for a snowman.

He swept them on to the snowman's head and around his neck, and stepped back to admire the results. 'Perfect.'

We stood looking at the snowman for a little while, sipping hot chocolate in the cold afternoon air.

'Funny how only *we* got the snow,' I said suddenly.

'Yeah . . .' Will said, giving Nick a tiny glance. He looked away as soon as he saw me notice.

Nick had his arms folded, check shirt sleeves rolled to the elbows to show off his reindeer tattoos. He had a little smile hiding somewhere in his beard. 'I've heard it can happen,' he said. 'Perhaps an aeroplane was flying overhead, and caused some sort of cloud disturbance.'

I remembered the sound of jingling bells from last night. *Perhaps it wasn't a* plane *flying overhead,* I thought. *Maybe it was something else flying entirely . . .*

# Nine

Meanwhile, at school, things were moving into that wonderful pre-Christmas zone where teachers put a film on during the afternoon and all the work is somehow connected to a festive theme. Our main focus was the Christmas play. We usually did a plain old Nativity, but our new drama teacher, Mr Beaumont, was one of those teachers who is Super Keen at all times, and he'd had the idea to do what he called a 'Rock & Roll Nativity'. The three Wise Men had inflatable electric guitars, Mary and Joseph were down-on-their-luck singers and the Angel Gabriel was a music business manager.

I was playing a sheep.

Before you start feeling sorry for me, someone has to be the sheep in every Nativity play, and it's usually me. I actually don't mind as it means you don't have to sing or dance, and I'm no good at either of those things (unless the dancing is copying the Rainbow Catz dance moves in my bedroom). Plus the costume is nice and warm.

Since we were doing such a high-tech production, and our primary school is so small, the local secondary school had been roped in to help, which meant I was seeing more of Will than I was used to. He was assisting with the lighting, doing something complicated with a tablet and lots of buttons. A bunch of his friends were also there – I recognised a few of them, Henry Martin in particular – but none of them seemed to be speaking to Will, who was instead spending a lot of time with the teacher who'd brought them over.

I kept an eye on my brother during the rehearsal. At one point I noticed him try to say something to Henry, but his friend went red and scuttled off like he was embarrassed to be noticed.

What was going on?

'Alright,' Mr Beaumont called when we had finished the run-through. 'Now, at the end of the play, there will be applause and cheering and so on . . . and that's when Father Christmas comes in to give out candy canes to the audience.' He gestured towards the back of the room, where Mr Melnyk, the caretaker, was standing wearing a rather threadbare Santa costume and a fake beard that didn't touch his chin. He wasn't smiling, and I got the feeling he'd been bullied into wearing the outfit.

'I am sure someone else can do this better than me,' he said wearily.

'Nonsense, you look fabulous,' Mr Beaumont replied, waving his hand as if to dismiss the idea. 'So, forwards Mr Melnyk, that's right, and give out the candy canes to the audience.'

Blushing redder than the tatty Santa suit, Mr Melnyk shuffled forwards a bit and meekly pretended to give out sweets to an invisible audience.

'Can't you put a bit more life into it?' Mr Beaumont said after a moment of slightly deflating Santa activity. 'A bit of *ho ho ho* or something?'

'I'm not an actor,' Mr Melnyk snapped. He stopped halfway down the aisle of chairs and looked pleadingly at Mr Beaumont. 'You need someone with . . . Santa experience.'

'Unfortunately, the chap I'd originally asked to do it has been snapped up by the shopping centre,' Mr Beaumont sighed. 'I'm sorry, but people born to play Santa Claus don't just wander across my path on a daily basis.'

Everyone jumped when a *buzz* sounded from the office security door. After a pause, the door opened remotely as the visitor was granted entrance.

My heart sank when I saw who it was.

Nick.

Nick, dressed in his red and tartan work clothes, his grey-white beard and hair flyaway in the cold December wind . . . holding leaflets about the farm park. He must have come to drop them off at school. He caught sight of me and Will and his face lit up in a smile. 'Oh, hello, Harper, Will!'

Will raised a hand while I tried to shrink down into the neck of my sheep costume.

Mr Beaumont, however, was looking at Nick as though he'd ridden down from heaven on a sunbeam. He walked over, a hand outstretched to shake. 'I'm Adam Beaumont,' he said quickly, seizing Nick's hand. 'Drama teacher.'

'I'm Nick. I'm Harper and Will's, er . . .' His voice trailed off awkwardly. 'I mean, their mum and I . . .'

Fortunately, Mr Beaumont didn't seem to care how that sentence was going to finish. 'Tell me, sir, have you ever been on stage at all? I think you'd make a *terrific* Father Christmas!'

'Er . . .' Nick looked a bit uncertain.

'You're meant for this part,' Mr Melnyk added, looking very relieved. He handed Nick the floppy Santa hat. 'Trust me.'

Nick tried to give the hat back. 'But I—'

'Nonsense.' Mr Beaumont waved a dismissive hand. 'I must *insist* you play the part of Father Christmas in our school play. You'd be doing a wonderful thing for the school, and the community.'

'Well . . . what do Harper and Will think to it?' Nick looked at us.

*No way*! I wanted to say, but Will spoke first.

'I don't mind,' he shrugged. 'Whatever.'

'There you are, then!' Mr Beaumont declared, without waiting for me to answer. 'Let's get you sorted at the office . . .' and he steered Nick into the Reception area.

Everyone started chatting as soon as they'd gone, saying how lucky it was that we had someone who looked the part, and how good it was that poor Mr Melnyk would be spared having to dress up. I sat with a plastic smile on my face, thinking that seeing Nick in an actual Santa Suit, giving out gifts, was *not* going to help me forget my theory.

'He'll make a good Santa, won't he, Henry?' I heard Will ask.

Henry didn't look at him. 'I guess.'

Will's shoulders slumped, and I realised I needed to get to the bottom of what was bothering my brother, before it got worse.

# Ten

We always have to get up extra-early on Wednesdays, because that's the day Mum starts work early and she drops us off at Breakfast Club on the way. But this Wednesday I wasn't woken up by Mum opening the curtains – I was jolted from sleep by a thunderous banging noise coming from downstairs.

My first thought was that there'd been an earthquake. Then that Mum had finally exploded the oven with one of her cooking experiments. But then I realised it was someone knocking endlessly and almost desperately on the front door.

I heard Mum go and answer it, her voice low even though the whole street was probably awake by now.

'Yes, Mrs Gupta?' She was using her very calm tone of voice, the one that usually means she's about to go completely bananas. 'You do realise it's 5 a.m.?'

'I'm sorry,' Mrs Gupta bellowed at a volume that could've woken the dead, 'but I was leaving for work and I saw it . . . it's on your *roof*!'

'What is?'

I heard the front door close – Mum must have gone outside to see what Mrs Gupta meant. There was a pause, and then the front door was wrenched open again and Mum burst back inside, now clearly on the phone.

'. . . I don't know how it got there! . . . Well, should I ring the RSPCA, or the fire brigade? . . . Alright, I'll wait for you.' She gave an irritated sigh through her teeth.

There was no point pretending to be asleep any more.

84

I went into the hallway and leaned over the landing rail. 'What's going on?'

Mum looked up at me with the sort of expression that said she'd much rather be in bed than having to deal with this. 'There's . . . a problem with the roof,' she said finally.

'Oh.' I didn't mention I'd heard Mrs Gupta say there was something *on* the roof. 'Is it going to fall in?'

'No! Well, I don't think so . . .' She looked at her phone. 'Nick's coming back from work to help.'

'Nick? Why? Is he going to borrow a ladder or something?' Will asked, coming out of his room wearing his old My Little Gremlins dressing gown over his Bert the Bear pyjamas. I was suddenly reminded that until very recently, Will had been interested in all the same things I was, before he morphed into a teenager.

'A ladder? No, it's just . . . something he thinks he can help with.' Mum ran her hands through her hair distractedly. 'I need to call work. We're going to be late.

Please can you both get ready to go, so we can leave as soon as this is sorted? And . . . stay inside.'

Will and I left her to it, having a quick and silent fight about who was going to use the bathroom first. When we were both dressed in our school uniform and making breakfast, Nick let himself in through the back door. His usually jolly face looked slightly anxious.

'What's going on?' Will asked as he stacked a fifth Weetabix into his bowl.

'Nothing we can't handle,' Nick said distractedly. His longish hair was escaping from the bun at the back of his head, as if he'd got ready in a rush. He switched the kettle on. 'It seems like a much bigger problem than it actually is.'

'What is it?' I asked. 'Has the chimney stack come down?'

'Oh, nothing that terrible,' Nick said. He poured hot water into an empty mug and stirred it as if he was thinking about something else. I opened my mouth to tell him he'd forgotten a tea bag but he had already wandered back out of the door to where Mum was standing in the garden, looking up at the roof.

Will nudged me. 'Are we going out or what?'

'Mum told us to stay inside,' I said piously. Then, grinning, I got up, Will on my heels as we went out into the garden.

Mum and Nick were talking together, quick and quiet, as though worried someone would overhear them.

'What's happening?' Will asked loudly, making them both jump. A bit of liquid splashed out of Nick's mug, and I saw and smelled that it was hot chocolate. Which didn't make any sense at all, because he'd forgotten to add anything to the mug before pouring in the water, hadn't he?

'Just − go back in,' Mum flapped at Will. 'I'll take you to school in a bit, after . . .'

But it was too late. Will had stepped back into the garden to see the roof of the house properly and was gawping up at it, mouth open, arms hanging by his sides like someone had cut his puppet-strings. 'What the . . . ?'

I'm a lot shorter than Will, so I had to dance back further into the garden to see, but when I finally looked up and saw the roof properly, my brain refused to believe what my eyes were seeing.

It was ridiculous.

It was impossible.

It was a reindeer . . . on the roof.

# Eleven

We all stood in the garden, staring up at the reindeer. The reindeer on the roof. The reindeer – antlers, bells and everything – just right up there on the roof of our house.

'How?' Will managed to speak first. 'But . . . how?'

'It flew,' I replied. 'Obviously.'

'Don't be silly,' Mum said, weakly.

Nick didn't say anything, he just stared up at the reindeer as if he was worried it would disappear if he stopped looking at it.

'Reindeer . . . on the roof.' Will folded his arms. 'Sure, why not.'

'We need to get it down before someone rings the papers or the TV people,' Mum said. 'This is ridiculous.'

'But how did it *get* there?' Will demanded.

Nick cleared his throat. 'Reindeer live in naturally craggy and rocky terrain,' he said in a very calm voice. 'What might seem like an impossible climb to you is nothing to a reindeer.'

I looked at him. Did he honestly expect any of us to believe that?

But Mum and Will seemed to accept it. 'Should I call the fire brigade?' Mum asked.

Nick took a sip of his hot chocolate. 'I think we'll have to,' he said. 'I can't see how else we're going to get her down . . .' He hesitated, as if he wanted to say something else, but had cut himself off.

'I hope they've got a crane,' Will said, as Mum dialled 999. 'It's a big animal.'

'Fire brigade, please,' Mum said into her phone. There was a pause, and then: 'Hello, yes. We've got an animal stuck on the roof, and I didn't know who else to call. Yes, on the roof of our house. No, no, it's not a cat,' she winced. 'It's a reindeer.'

\*

The fire brigade thought it was hilarious.

'We rescue stuck cats all the time,' the Chief said, grinning as he took pictures on his phone, 'but this is one for our hall of fame.'

'Please don't put our house on social media,' Mum cringed.

'Don't worry, Dr Hall, we're professionals.'

Up on the roof, two firefighters were trying to work out the best way to get a massive harness around a reindeer. The reindeer was watching them with what can only be described as cool contempt.

'Do we go through the legs, or what, Chief?' one of the firefighters yelled.

'I'm a bit worried about the horns, myself,' the second one added.

Nick was rubbing his hands together worriedly. 'Antlers, not horns. And yes, get the fabric on her tummy and fasten the straps over her back.'

Will took a loud bite of toast. He'd brought a stack out to eat whilst he watched the fun. 'Watch she doesn't try to fly away,' he said, mouth full of jam.

The firefighters laughed, but none of our family did.

On the roof, the two firefighters managed to fix a sort of hammock around the reindeer, and clip straps around her back. The animal was quite placid about the whole thing, only gently nibbling at the uniforms of the two women who were trying to help, and looking curiously down at us as if unable to understand why we were staring at her.

Once she was strapped in, the firefighter closest to the edge of the roof gave a wave. 'Bring the lift over!' she shouted.

The lift – a sort of cage on the end of a massive robotic arm that came from the back of the fire engine – was driven close. There was plenty of room for two people and a reindeer to fit, and the animal walked into it quite happily, as if she did this sort of thing every day.

The firefighters gave the thumbs up, and everyone cheered and applauded as the lift came slowly down, bringing all three occupants back to Earth.

'Well done, everyone,' the Chief said as the reindeer was unclipped. 'Excellent work.'

The reindeer, as soon as she was free, trotted straight over to Nick and started sniffing and nuzzling his coat as if looking for treats

'Well, she knows who her keeper is,' one of the firefighters said. She took her helmet off. 'How did she even get up there?'

'Excellent climbers, reindeer,' Nick said, fussing the animal's head. I saw on her bell-covered harness that her name was Meteor. 'Thank you so much for all your help.'

'Not a problem, makes a change from cats. But what would she have climbed—'

Meteor decided to change the subject by suddenly doing an enormous poo. Everyone recoiled in horror, while Mum mumbled something about it being good for the garden roses, at least.

The fire brigade didn't linger for long after the stink-bomb was dropped. They thanked Nick for the adventure and told Mum to call again if she had any more animals on the roof, before driving away, giving us cheerful waves as they turned at the end of the street.

'Right, stinky lady, let's get you home,' Nick said to Meteor, who was looking very pleased with herself.

'Do you need a horse-box?' Mum asked. 'They have emergency ones at the vet's surgery.'

'We'll walk,' Nick said firmly. 'She needs a talking to.'

I gave Will a meaningful look. *A talking to?* I mouthed. He shrugged.

'I'll let you know when we get back,' Nick said to Mum. He took hold of Meteor's harness. 'Come on, madam.'

Meteor trotted happily beside him, and the rest of us were left to try and get to school on time.

The pile of poo stayed in the middle of the garden.

# Twelve

The one good thing about the 'escaped' reindeer was that Nick had to stay in the farm park to help reinforce the fences and couldn't come to the practices for the Rock & Roll Nativity play. Having him hanging around at home all the time was quite enough for me without having to see him at school too.

It was all going pretty well at practice. On Tuesday there was a small disaster in rehearsals when one of the backing singers/angels forgot all their words and ran off the stage, but other than that everyone was

97

feeling prepared. Even the breakdancing shepherds were great.

Will and his classmates were still working on the tech side of things. I kept half an eye on my brother as he tried to talk to the others a few times. Most of them were casually friendly, but Henry was ignoring him powerfully, and it was his attitude that was affecting the other boys.

I wanted to give Henry a good poke at the back of the head, but that probably wasn't going to help.

I hung back when we were dismissed, taking my time with my coat so I could watch Will and his friends – or *not* friends.

Will was swapping his school shoes for his trainers, when one of the bigger kids from Year Nine shoved his head down and made him nearly fall off the bench. Will stood up immediately and got right up in front of them, shouting something that, if Mum asks, I don't know the meaning of.

The older boys clearly didn't expect this response; they stepped back and said something back to Will whilst gesturing at the others in their group. Will is tall for his age and pretty tough, so they soon turned away. Will stared after them until they went around the corner and then kicked the metal waste-bin, hard. It went *CLANG* and he immediately started hopping about on the other foot, wincing.

'Are you OK?' I ran over to him.

'No, I think I've broken my toe.' Will hopped around a bit more before deciding he was fine.

'No, but really . . . *are* you OK?' I asked again.

He gave me the sort of withering look only big brothers can manage. 'I'm fine.'

'But those boys—'

'Are idiots,' Will finished for me. 'Don't worry about it, Harper.'

'But – but you and Henry . . .'

Will gave a tiny cringe, but managed to hide it. 'I said, *don't worry about it.*'

'Have you had an argument?' I carried on. 'He's not been round for ages.'

'Harper, please.' Will suddenly looked very tired. 'Just leave it.'

'Fine, but this isn't over,' I said, pointing at my eyes with two fingers, and then at his. 'I'm going to get to the bottom of this.'

'I'm sure you are,' he grumbled, then took out his phone and started swiping through PuzzoCube practice slides. Even when he didn't have the toy with him it was never far from his mind.

We left school and started the walk home. The air was that horrible mixture of damp and cold, and it found its way inside my shoes so my feet were blocks of ice by the time we got back. Mum was home, and the roof was thankfully free of reindeer, so we went straight inside – and almost broke our necks falling over a collection of boxes and bags piled up just inside the hallway.

'What's all this?' I called as Will picked himself up, turning a huge grey sack over to look at it. It had a Royal Mail stamp on it. 'Mum, what *have* you been ordering?'

Mum came into the hall, smiling. 'Oh, it's all for Nick. His post has been redirected here while he's staying with us.'

'Is he moonlighting as a postie?' Will asked, picking up a box to read the front. 'Where's this even from? It's not in English.'

'Some of it will be from Finland, for the reindeer.' Mum pointed to the airmail stamp. 'See? Don't worry, he'll take what he needs back to the farm park with him. How was practice?'

Will followed Mum inside, telling her about the tech problems they were having, but I was distracted by the heaps of parcels and bags. Who got *this* much post all in one go? And the boxes were one thing, but the sacks didn't look like they'd hold anything for the reindeer – they were full of something crinkly and crackly . . .

Checking that no one was looking, I carefully undid one of the grey Royal Mail sacks and slipped a hand into the tiny opening I made at the top.

I pulled my hand back out, fingers closed around something thin and sharp and flat. A *letter*.

My hands were shaking. I turned the letter over, not knowing what to expect. Not daring to hope, not daring to believe what I might see written for a name and address . . .

And it was in another language. I couldn't even sound out the words because I didn't recognise some of the letters; they weren't from the alphabet I was used to. It could have been addressed to anyone, anywhere.

'Harper, come and help your brother set the table,'
Mum called.

Disappointed, I went to slide the letter back into the
sack, until I spotted a word at the very bottom of the
address – one I *did* recognise:

*Lapland*.

# Thirteen

Those first boxes and sacks of letters were just the start.

As soon as Nick removed the parcels and post from our house, more arrived. Every delivery service, every courier, every person in a white van came to our front door carrying great big bags of Airmail and huge boxes that were sealed shut, and once a gigantic wooden crate that didn't fit through the door and had to wait outside for Nick to come and collect it.

'Sorry about all this,' he said, picking the crate up in his bare hands and lifting it into his pickup truck without any effort (which was weird, because the guys who delivered it had to use a special lift for especially heavy packages to unload it). 'I'll soon have this out of your way.'

I scrutinised every single box I could get close to – which wasn't many because Mum was always tidying them away if Nick wasn't there to immediately take them out of the house, but they were always the same – letters and alphabets I didn't recognise, stamps with flags I had no clue about, with even the addressee being a mystery.

'You must have been good this year if you're getting all these presents!' the postie laughed one morning, as she handed over another four boxes from the back of her red van.

Mum laughed back, signing for the parcels as if this was all perfectly normal. 'It's my boyfriend,' she said, and I cringed. 'He's having to have stuff for work sent here for the time being.'

'Ah, I see.'

I didn't see. No one who worked at a petting zoo could possibly be getting this amount of post unless they were running a farm for a million reindeer. But there was no way to be sure.

Until a few days later, when I had a brainwave.

'What are you up to, Harps?' Mum asked as she and Nick came into the kitchen to start making dinner.

'Writing a letter,' I said, keeping my eyes on the paper.

'Oh? To who?'

I looked up, right at them both. 'To Father Christmas.'

They both smiled, identical 'isn't that sweet' smiles that could have been copied right out of a picture book. Nick actually gave a little chuckle.

'That's lovely, Harper,' Mum said, starting to root around for pots and pans. 'What are you asking for?'

'You'll see if I get it,' I said, looking back at my letter.

'You're not going to tell me?' Mum asked, sounding surprised.

'Parents don't need to see the letters, do they?' Nick said seriously. 'It's Santa delivering the presents, after all.'

'Exactly,' I said. I started to fold it up to slide the paper into the envelope I'd specially decorated with every feather, sparkle and piece of glitter I could get my hands on. The envelope was practically encrusted with jewels. If the letters arriving at our house were for Santa, this was the perfect plan to prove it – spotting my envelope through one of those pale grey mail sacks would be easy.

'That's very fancy,' Nick said admiringly. 'He won't miss that one.'

'Does he ever miss one?' I asked, forcing my letter into the glue-stiffened envelope.

'Never.'

I looked up into Nick's beard. 'You sure?'

The faintest twinkle – so brief and bright that I wasn't sure it had been there at all – glinted in Nick's eyes, before he gave a nod. 'I'm sure.'

I started to glue the envelope flap down, my mind whirling. It was strange. Half the time Nick was around, the whole Santa Theory seemed too far-fetched to be true. But the rest of the time it seemed like the only possible explanation.

Did I really want Nick to be Santa? Was I ready to have a stepdad who flew a sleigh? Was I ready for a stepdad at all?

Ready or not, I'd written the letter now. I just needed to post it.

'Where does Santa live?' I asked.

'The North Pole,' said Mum.

'Lapland,' said Nick.

'Another world, I think,' said Will, coming into the kitchen with his eyes firmly fixed on his PuzzoCube. He navigated the furniture without looking up, pulling out and settling down on to a chair in a fluid movement that required no hands whatsoever. His tablet was running a timer as it displayed what looked like a very complicated pattern for him to copy on his cube.

I wrote all three locations down just to be sure.

'Everyone likes curry, yes?' Mum asked, taking jars and spices down from the cupboard.

Me and Will exchanged worried glances. Mum's curries had been known to cause pans to melt and the wallpaper to change colour.

Nick must have seen our expressions because he said, 'Why don't I help? I know a fantastic new recipe . . .' and together the cooking became less of a science experiment and more of a delicious-smelling process that had all of us waiting eagerly for the meal to be ready.

'Don't people eat reindeer?' Will asked when we were all finally sitting at the table and his plate was passed over.

'Probably,' Mum said with a sigh. She's been vegan for twenty years. 'No food with a face' is what she always says.

'It's quite common in Arctic cultures,' Nick said. 'The people who keep reindeer for those purposes use every part of the animal. The meat, the furs, the antlers . . . nothing goes to waste. The furs are fantastic at keeping you warm, even in the coldest places on Earth.'

'I'd love to go to the Arctic one day,' Mum said. 'Go see the Northern Lights, make friends with a penguin . . .'

'Penguins live at the South Pole, Mum,' Will said.

'Oh.'

'The Northern Lights are beautiful,' Nick said. 'Like ribbons of energy hanging in the sky. They paint themselves across the darkness, all greens and blues, pinks and golds, shimmering and waving silently between the stars. And you feel so small as you look up from the white under your boots to the colours in the sky . . . the world feels enormous, and like anything could happen.

111

Anything at all . . .' He stopped as he realised all of us were staring at him. 'It's very nice,' he said, blushing.

'You make it sound like magic,' Mum said.

He nodded. 'Oh, it definitely is. Trust me.'

# Fourteen

'What if he actually is, though?' I whispered to Will.

We were in his smelly bedroom, because Will said my Rainbow Catz posters made his eyes hurt, watching a video about the Northern Lights. Will was only half-watching, twisting his PuzzoCube around and around, working out the best combinations.

'He isn't,' he replied, as if that was the end of the conversation.

I couldn't leave it alone. 'But Will . . . look at all the clues. The reindeer, the post, the way he knows about the Arctic . . .'

113

Will sighed, and resumed his puzzling. 'I know, Harps. I know.'

'So?' I prompted. 'What other explanation is there?'

Will gave a huge sigh. 'I don't know. But it can't possibly be true. It's childish to even think it. Plus, *if* I decided I *did* believe that our new stepdad is Santa, and then he turns out not to be . . .' Will shrugged. 'The disappointment would be too much right now, anyway.'

I realised something. 'Because you're already disappointed in Henry?'

Will's fingers slipped on the smooth edges of the puzzle. 'Um. Yeah.'

'What did he do?'

'It's nothing he's said. Just . . . his behaviour.'

'I thought he was nice?'

'He is. Most of the time.' Will completed his puzzle and held it up to the light as if trying to see through it.

I could tell he didn't want to say anything else, so I just squeezed his arm.

*

Will wasn't in the mood for talking the next day – he was endlessly playing practice rounds of PuzzleCube in preparation for the big competition at the weekend. Even the new PlayStation sat forgotten as he twisted and rearranged the pieces of the cube over and over, so fast it made my eyes blur to watch him.

Once a year, people from all over the country who liked these 1970s cubes would get together for a tournament, and Will had entered a time-trial to try to win a thousand pounds. He didn't fancy his chances, as there were people who'd been playing the cubes for fifty years, but the runner-up prizes were good too.

'You'll strain your fingers,' Mum said half-heartedly as Will kept one eye on his tablet and one hand on his cube during dinner. She didn't like to complain too much;

115

it was unusual for Will to be this distracted and she knew the competition meant a lot to him.

'Where did you get that anyway?' Nick asked, peering at it.

'Found it at a jumble sale,' Will said proudly as he twisted the cube. 'They haven't made them for ages.'

'Ah.' Nick looked sort of amused as he went back to his food. 'It's wonderful how you can always discover something new, even if the new thing is something old.'

Will gave a sideways sort of smile.

At bedtime, Mum confiscated the cube and the tablet, saying Will needed his sleep. 'Look well if you fall asleep during the competition,' she said, smiling.

He pulled a face, but didn't argue. The contest meant more to him than Christmas.

*

The next day was wet from overnight rain, and the air was thick and soupy like we were due a good

116

thunderstorm. I was glad it was Friday – I wanted the weekend off from sheep practice.

Will and I were walking home. Will had managed to cajole Mum into letting him take his cube to school in his bag. I think he liked knowing he had it with him, like a sort of lucky charm.

Ahead of us, walking on his own, was Henry. I glared at the back of his headphone-wearing head. I wasn't sure what he'd done to upset my brother, but he was now Harper's Enemy Number One.

Will wasn't glaring, though. He just looked a bit sad.

Henry pulled his phone out of his pocket as he got close to the edge of the pavement, glanced up, then made to cross over, stepping straight out into the road.

I didn't really see what happened.

I felt, rather than saw, Will shove past me and run into the road. I heard the scream of car brakes, a thud, a gasp from other people on the pavement, a yell as something soft hit the ground.

About one second had passed.

I blinked to see Will and Henry sprawled in the middle of the road. I was frozen in place, wanting to run over but unable to make my legs work and then . . . the boys moved. They slowly got to their feet, with skinned hands and ripped trousers but otherwise unharmed. The car that would have hit Henry had stopped a few metres ahead of them. The driver, white as a sheet, opened his door and stepped out. Where the car had braked hard was a flattened, torn mess of school bag. Will's school bag. He must have dropped it when he pushed Henry out of the way.

My brain unfroze. 'Will!'

He raised a hand to me. He was OK. He helped Henry, who looked as if he was in shock, over to the side of the road. His headphones were still playing loudly, I could hear the beat in the silence of the aftermath.

Henry gawped at my brother. 'You just . . .' His eyes drifted to Will's destroyed backpack. 'Oh no, Will.'

Will tore himself away from Henry and darted to his bag. The whole thing had been steamrollered. He picked it up and hunted through it, searching desperately . . .

. . . and drew out his beloved PuzzoCube.

The car had driven straight over it. The middle was completely crushed, the edges bulging with cogs and broken plastic like the cube was a sandwich someone had pressed their hand down on, making all the filling spill out.

It was well and truly broken.

'Will, I'm really sorry,' Henry was saying. 'I should have looked where I was going—'

'Not your fault.' Will just stared at his ruined toy. 'It's OK.'

'Maybe it can be fixed?' Henry looked doubtfully at the smashed puzzle.

'It's OK,' Will said again, in a hollow sort of voice. 'I'm just glad it wasn't you that got flattened.' He looked into Henry's face. Henry went red. 'Come on, Harps,' he said to me.

And I followed him up the road, carrying what was left of his bag, as Will cradled his broken puzzle in his hands.

# Fifteen

The puzzle cube sat in the middle of the table like a disassembled rainbow.

The mechanism was completely crushed, the plastic moving parts had come apart and the little coloured squares were peeling off.

'Maybe you could find another one?' I suggested, after half an hour of staring at it with Will.

He shook his head. 'They don't make them any more. That's why one of the entry rules for the tournament is bringing your own with you.' His chin was on the table,

121.

arms slumped downwards, utterly miserable. 'I can't believe this.'

'You saved Henry's life,' Mum said. She'd come home after hearing about the near-accident and had patched up Will's hands. She wasn't cross at all, just relieved everyone was alright. 'That silly boy! What was he thinking, stepping out into the road like that?'

Will just sighed. 'This is the worst day of my life.'

Mum stroked his hair. 'Can I do anything to help?'

'No,' Will said. 'I wish you could.' He sounded defeated.

The back door clicked open and Nick let himself in. He was beaming from ear to ear, but the smile dropped off his face when he saw the sadness in the room. 'Is everything alright?' he asked.

Mum quickly explained what had happened with Henry, the car, and Will's bravery that had cost him his puzzle championship goal.

Nick looked upset. 'It's such a shame that your reward for being so brave is so terrible,' he said, looking at the broken puzzle. His bright dark eyes flicked over the components, from shattered plastic to twisted mechanism. 'Very unfair. Do you suppose it could be fixed?'

'No, and definitely not by tomorrow,' Will said. He pointed out the little smiley face someone, decades ago, had scratched into the plastic surround. 'Not so happy now, are you?'

Nick gave a sad sort of laugh. He reached across the table for the puzzle. 'Can I see it? I might be able to fix it.'

Will snorted. 'Good luck. The casing is ruined and that's before we even talk about the mechanism.'

Nick lifted the twisted toy and brought it close to his face, frowning as he examined it, like a jeweller looking at a diamond to see how much it might be worth. 'I've got a lot of experience in the area of fixing toys,' he said. 'Would you let me at least try?'

'Sure.' Will shrugged, lifting his face off the table. 'You can't break it any worse by trying to fix it, after all.'

'Give me until tomorrow morning,' Nick said, with a certainty that made us all blink in surprise. 'Trust me.'

*

Will went to bed early, saying he was too depressed to stay up. Nick sat at the kitchen table, examining the puzzle cube for hours, but didn't seem to be trying to make any repairs. Will was probably right – it was broken beyond fixing.

The Christmas tree lights cast colourful patterns over the ceiling and walls as me and Mum watched *The Great Christmas Wrapping Competition* on TV. We each had a tiny chocolate reindeer to eat, but the Christmas spirit wasn't there. Both of us felt too sorry for Will.

'I wonder why Will fell out with Henry in the first place,' I said.

Mum looked away guiltily.

'You know?!'

She pulled a face like she was thinking about how much to tell me. 'It's Will's business,' she said after a moment. 'And if he hasn't told you, I'm not sure I should speak for him.'

'But I don't understand,' I said. 'They were best friends.'

'Sometimes,' Mum said carefully, 'even best friends have rough patches. I'm sure if they talked, they'd realise they're the same boys they've always been. It's just a misunderstanding.'

I certainly didn't understand, but Mum kept distracting me by talking about the wrapping on telly, so I didn't get a chance to ask again.

Nick poked his head around the door. 'I'm going to tuck the girls in for the night,' he said, meaning that he was going to make sure the petting zoo reindeer were safely in the barn (and not on anyone's roof). 'I'll be back later. Good night, Harper. See you in the morning.'

'See you,' I said, not bothering to ask whether he'd fixed the puzzle cube. It would take a miracle to mend it, after all.

Me and Mum stayed up a little longer until the latest contestant was eliminated from the Christmas wrapping competition, and then it was time for me to go to bed.

I walked past the dining table on my way to the stairs. The puzzle cube was gone. Nick must have taken it with him.

As I passed Will's room I gave his door a little pat in sympathy.

Maybe things would look better in the morning.

# Sixteen

I was woken the next morning by a yell that shook the entire house.

I jumped out of bed, ready to do something, but not sure what. Maybe there was another reindeer on the roof. Maybe it had snowed three metres deep overnight. Maybe there was a sleigh parked next to Mum's battered old car.

Actually, it was none of those things.

I pelted downstairs in my pyjamas and dressing gown to find Mum and Will staring at something on the table.

'What's going on?' I asked.

'Just *look* at it,' Will said hoarsely.

He stepped aside so I could see. There, in the middle of the table, sitting on a neat little nest of straw, was Will's puzzle cube. Mended. Looking for all the world like it had never been broken at all.

'It's a new one,' I said. It was the only possible explanation.

'It's not.' Will pointed to the smiley face someone had etched into the plastic. 'Look at that. It's mine. It's the same cube.' He picked it up like it was a crystal swan.

'It can't be fixed?' I couldn't believe it. 'But it was all smashed. How . . . ?'

Mum shrugged and smiled. 'Nick said he was good at fixing toys.'

The realisation thumped into my chest. *Of course* Nick was good at fixing toys. Because he was Santa Claus.

'So, the reindeer, the snow, the fixing toys, the cookies,

the white beard . . . no one else thinks it's all just a little bit too much of a coincidence?' I asked, my voice going all high-pitched and weird.

'Oh shush,' Mum said absent-mindedly, tidying away the little straw nest.

But Will gave me a look. A look I hadn't seen before. His talk the other night about not wanting to believe . . . well, it seemed that right now he couldn't *not* believe it. His precious puzzle cube was fixed, he was going to his competition, all because of a miracle performed by a man who just might be . . . just possibly was . . .

We couldn't talk about it right then though; Mum was buzzing about getting breakfasts and talking about what time she and Will needed to leave to go to the community hall for the PuzzoCube tournament. My brother and I gave each other the side-eye, and a silent promise to get back to this later.

Right now, all that mattered was Will getting ready, and acing his chance to win.

*

We arrived at the community hall and got Will checked in. He had a lanyard and a badge and was carrying his puzzle cube in a sort of special travel box. We wished him luck and promised to pick him up at the end of the day.

'What shall we do together?' Mum asked as we drove off.

'Something Christmassy,' I said. 'I feel really Christmassy again, now!'

'Oh, let's bake gingerbread,' Mum said. 'I love how it makes the house smell delicious.'

'Gingerbread houses,' I said. 'Then we'll have a big house that smells delicious and a small house that tastes delicious!' We'd never made one and I'd always wanted to.

'Wonderful idea.' Mum pulled into the supermarket so we could grab the ingredients. 'Shall I ask Nick to help?'

'Isn't he at work?' I said, my enthusiasm slipping a bit. I wanted Mum to myself for a change. I always had to share her, whether it was with Will, her work, or now with Nick.

'He's only there until three, today.' She must have picked up on my mood though, because she added: 'But let's do it just the two of us. Now − what sweets do you want to decorate with?'

There was more maths involved with the gingerbread house than I usually liked to do when baking. Mum cut out paper shapes for us to use as a model for the sides and roof of the house, and we placed those on top of the rolled-out dough. Then we used a flat knife to trace around the paper to make the correct shape for the 3D jigsaw. But when the dough slabs came out of the oven they had transformed from nice flat shapes to wobbly blobs that looked nothing like a side of a house.

'Maybe they'll look better when they're all stuck together,' Mum said uncertainly, opening a tin of chickpeas. She was going to use the liquid from the can to help make a vegan royal icing for the edible glue.

The gingerbread pieces were so misshapen that we had to use tons of royal icing to get them to all stick together, and then Mum had to stand holding it all in place whilst we waited for it to set. I gave her a drink with a straw and we both had to laugh when the doorbell went and it was the postie with another load of boxes and sacks of post for Nick.

'You look like you're having fun,' she said as she brought the bags into the hall.

'We're making a gingerbread house,' I explained.

'That would be the lovely smell, then. Are you all

sorted for Christmas?' She gave me her machine to sign for the post since Mum couldn't move.

'No,' Mum called through. 'We don't have a nut roast or anything. I've not even written any cards.'

'Don't bother,' the postie said. 'I've got enough to deliver as it is.' She wished us happy baking, and I went back to rescue Mum, whose arms were getting tired.

'I think it's set,' she said, lifting her hands away carefully. 'Time for decorating?'

Decorating was messy. After three minutes, both of us were covered in chocolate, sugar, icing, pink food colouring, sweets, that weird sour dipping dust, and edible glitter. The gingerbread house looked as though a fairy unicorn had done a huge sparkly sweetie candy cane poo right on top of it.

'We could totally go on that baking show,' Mum said, eating some of the raw leftover dough with a wooden spoon. 'That's a work of art.'

'It's a work of something,' I said, taking a picture of it. The flash on my tablet went off, and, as if it had been waiting for the right moment, the gingerbread house shuddered and collapsed into a pile of broken biscuit walls and sugar decorations.

I looked at Mum, and Mum looked at me, and then we both exploded into a fit of giggles. She came over and gave me a massive hug.

'Shall we just eat it?' she asked.

'Definitely,' I said, crying with laughter.

Mum kissed the top of my head and went to put the kettle on.

We collected Will from the community hall a couple of hours later – he hadn't won the thousand pounds, but he had won the Junior Championship Award, which was a family pass to Alton Towers.

We sang daft Christmas songs all the way home in the car and, when we arrived back, Nick was already there.

He was just putting the finishing touches to a gingerbread *castle*, and had arranged our broken leftovers to be the castle garden decorations. I might have felt a bit put out that Nick had been successful after our spectacular failure, but he'd iced little biscuit people to look like me, Will, Mum and himself, and it looked so adorable I didn't even mind.

Nick did look slightly worried as Will came in, but Will didn't hesitate – he ran over to Nick and gave him the biggest hug I've ever seen Will give anybody. I felt like my heart was so full it might burst. Whether Nick was Santa or not – and I still had my suspicions – maybe having him around wasn't so bad.

# Seventeen

It was the Christmas play dress rehearsal. I was wearing an amazing sheep costume – Mum managed to get a fleece from one of the farmers she worked with, so my outfit had been upgraded and was incredibly realistic, even though the hooves were made out of yoghurt pots and the horns were kitchen roll tubes that had been twisted and painted.

Will was on the lighting deck at the back of the room, and the other older kids were backstage handling costume changes and curtains and so on. I spotted Henry glancing

137

at Will now and again with a bit of a sorry look on his face, but Will hadn't seemed to notice. He was still looking as pleased as Punch in the aftermath of his puzzle competition.

Mr Beaumont was darting about like he was directing a Hollywood movie, adjusting the Rockstar Wise Men's inflatable guitars and making sure the Angelic Agents' sunglasses were glittering in the huge overhead lights. To one side, Mary and Joseph were practising their rags-to-riches quick change for the 'Superstar over Bethlehem' number, and the doll playing the part of Baby Jesus was sitting in a manger covered in sparkles and foil.

Since Nick seemed to so *embody the essence of Santa Claus*, as Mr Beaumont put it, his role had been upgraded from just giving out candy canes to leading the choir and actors in the final songs of the play. Right now, Nick was sitting at the back of the room waiting for Mr Beaumont to give him his cue.

'Right, everyone, last big number,' Mr Beaumont yelled through cupped hands. 'We've seen the greatest story ever told and now it's time to have the big singalong.' He pointed with enthusiasm at the rear curtain and it dropped down to reveal the painted-on lyrics for 'A Very Rockin' Christmas'.

We all started to sing; we knew the words off by heart by this point in the practice and the actions were automatic. But it was a great song, and it made everyone laugh and smile as we sang about the magic of Christmas, friendship, love and eventually things like presents and . . . Santa Claus.

'Yes, that's your cue!' Mr Beaumont called to Nick, who stood up and picked up a soft-looking Santa hat and a sack.

And everything about him seemed to suddenly change.

There was a soft gasp from one of the donkeys next to me

Nick stood straighter, the sack slung over a shoulder, his stance at ease. The slightly moth-eaten hat on his head didn't look so dull or careworn any more, but instead full and fluffy. His blue and red tartan shirt didn't seem out of place, and neither did his braces or work-trousers. Out of nowhere, he'd transformed from a quiet man who'd been roped into taking part in a school play to someone who commanded the attention of the room. All the children in the hall stared as if recognising something about him that they had previously forgotten.

Mr Beaumont didn't seem to have noticed, however. 'And a bit of *ho ho ho*, if you please, a *Merry Christmas* and then hand out the sweeties.'

Nick gave a smile that seemed to light him up from the inside. 'HO HO HO!' he roared in a rolling laugh that echoed in the hall. 'Merry Christmas!' And he reached into the sack and started handing out toys.

'There's a jigsaw for you, Alice,' he said. 'And a football for you, Rafi. Lego for you, Joe, and a cuddly pig for you, Avery . . .'

'Wait a minute,' Avery said, holding on to his cuddly pig. 'Is this real? Can I keep it?'

It was as though he'd flicked a switch, and suddenly the magical mood vanished.

'Sorry,' said Mr Beaumont, 'Mr, er, Nick . . . did you put presents in that sack? It was supposed to be empty for the rehearsal.'

The festive joy radiating from Nick stopped and instantly he was just a man in a Santa hat again, holding an obviously empty sack. 'Oh,' he said, not missing a beat, 'I just thought . . . I'd bring them all a treat, since they've all been working so hard.' He reached into the sack and drew out a carrier bag full of small toys, as if it had been hiding inside the whole time. The shape of the sack hadn't changed at all.

Mr Beaumont tapped his chin with a finger. 'Oh. Well, that's very kind of you. But let's skip to the curtain call for now . . .'

Nick made his way to the front as the song changed to 'We Wish You A Merry Christmas', the one that we'd reappear to at the end to give our bows. Mr Beaumont waved his hands like an orchestra conductor, encouraging the imaginary audience of grown-ups to clap, and then, the play was over.

'Excellent work, everyone,' he said. 'I think we'll knock 'em dead tomorrow. Nick, are you sorted with your costume?'

'Yes, it's at the dry cleaners,' Nick said. He pulled the hat off his head, and his wispy grey-white hair stuck up a bit from the static.

'Lovely, lovely . . . Well, good night everyone. We'll see you all tomorrow night at six o'clock sharp!'

Nick looked up at this. 'Six?'

'A few minutes before, if you can,' Mr Beaumont said. 'Just to be on the safe side.'

'I have to make sure the reindeer are fed and watered first,' Nick said, looking thoughtful.

Despite my earlier reservations about Nick being involved in the play, my heart sank a little. There was no denying he made an excellent Santa Claus, and he really brought the whole play together. What if he couldn't come after all, and let everyone down?

But Nick was smiling. 'I'm sure I'll be able to make it on time. In fact, I promise to be here.' He caught my eye, and gave me a nod. I felt reassured at that – Nick didn't seem like the sort of man to break promises easily.

We packed the props and costumes away for the next day, making sure everything would be ready to go. Mr Beaumont dismissed us all, counting us out of the building. Will and I left with Nick, who was carrying his sack and hat in a bag-for-life.

It had been a damp and muggy December day, but as we stepped outside the evening air was sharp and biting. It smelled like snow.

'My word,' Mr Beaumont said as he locked the building. 'It's nippy out, all of a sudden. Maybe we'll get a white Christmas.'

'I hope so,' Nick said. 'It's not festive without snow . . .' And as he spoke, a couple of tiny flakes drifted out of the dark night and swirled through the air. 'Started already,' he smiled.

Will and I shared a look. We both knew. Now, we had to decide what to do about it.

# Eighteen

It was the last day of school, and the day of the Christmas play. Lessons were suspended. Everyone watched films in the classroom, made crackers out of tissue paper and cardboard tubes, or helped with getting ready for the performance.

The chairs were set out, the lights double- and triple-tested, and Mr Beaumont was full of praise for everyone as we went through a few key scenes one last time. Everyone was there apart from Nick, who wouldn't arrive until the evening's performance. When the bell

145

rang at 3.30 p.m. we promised to be back in plenty of time to change into our costumes, and staggered out of the gates carrying all the arts and crafts we'd made over the past week. No doubt Mum would hang on to them until they disintegrated.

Mum got off work early enough to feed us frozen pizzas and change out of her scrubs and into her fanciest Christmas jumper, which was more sparkles than wool. She wrapped tinsel around her head like a halo, and helped Will fasten his tie and put on a pair of sunglasses patterned with candy cane stripes. My sheep costume was ready for me at school, and we decided to walk there to avoid a nightmare parking situation. The school had been built before cars were invented, and it was always a mad scramble to be as close as possible unless you walked.

Mr Beaumont was looking extremely harassed when we arrived, ticking me and Will off the list and directing Mum to the hall where the rest of the parents were waiting. 'Where's your other half?' he asked her as he showed her the way. 'He's our star for the finale.'

'He isn't here yet?' Mum asked, but then they went through the doorway and I didn't hear any more.

'Sounds like Nick hasn't turned up yet,' I said to Will worriedly.

'He will,' Will said. 'He won't let us down.' And we went off to get changed backstage.

But there was still no sign of Nick as the rest of the audience began to file in. I could see Mum in the front row, checking her phone now and again and glancing at the door at the back of the hall, but Nick hadn't appeared.

'What if he doesn't show up?' I whispered to Will backstage. 'He might not want the attention.'

'We'll have to get Mr Melnyk to do it after all.'

'But Nick has the costume. *And* the sack.' I pointed out.

Before Will could respond, he was pulled away to the lighting deck to begin the show, and there was no time left to even feel let down by Nick's absence.

Mr Beaumont swept onstage dressed as a huge Christmas pudding. 'Welcome, one and all, to our very special Christmas performance. I know you're all looking forward to seeing the show, so please turn off your devices and get ready for *A Very Rock and Roll Christmas*!'

There was applause, and the stage went dark as the music for the first number began to play.

'Where's your stepfather?' Mr Beaumont hissed at me as the Angel Gabriel swaggered onstage to tell Mary and Joseph they had been talent-scouted.

'He's not my stepfather,' I replied. 'And I don't know.'

Mr Beaumont took several deep, calming breaths. 'Oh well, the show must go on . . .' he said, slightly hysterically, before scuttling away to make sure Herod was ready for his solo.

I peeped back out at the stage. 'Come *on*, Nick,' I whispered to myself, my heart hurting. 'You promised us.'

The show did go on. The songs and dances were great, and I was a perfect sheep in the stable as Mary and Joseph were serenaded by the Wise Men. But as the story was coming to an end, a spike of panic began to nudge at me. Where was Nick? Was he really going to leave us like this? He'd promised to be here, and he was letting us down . . .

What sort of a maybe-one-day stepfather did that?

We all assembled on the stage, ready for the final number. The scroll with the lyrics rolled down over the curtain, inviting everyone to sing along. But the words stuck in my throat and my eyes were watering. I couldn't believe that Nick would—

The hall door burst open.

'Nick?' I looked up.

There, at the back of the hall, breathing heavily but dressed head to foot in a bright red and fluffy Santa costume, was Nick. He held the sack up and boomed: 'HO HO HO! MERRY CHRISTMAS!'

And everyone cheered.

Relief went through me like liquid sunshine, lighting me up and making me clap for joy. Everyone joined in, applauding the sight of Santa directing the choir with a candy cane and handing out more of them from the sack as he strode up and down.

As we all began to do our bows, Nick came up to stand next to me. I felt a warm happiness I hadn't associated with Nick before, and realised this must be how Will felt when he saw his cube was fixed. Happy for himself, but also happy that Nick was just *there*.

I was happy he was there too.

'Merry Christmas, everyone!'

# Nineteen

Mum finished work early on Christmas Eve and picked Will and me up from Busy Bee's School Holiday Club in the afternoon. The roads were jam-packed with people trying to get into town to do their last bits of shopping, find a frozen turkey, hunt down replacement bulbs for the fairy lights, or ask their grandmas for her secret gravy recipe. The view outside the car window was of the gloom that came with an early setting sun, a watery blur of headlights, Christmas tree decorations and flashing signs in shop windows. It was starting to sleet, the wet clumps melting before they hit the cars, making the underwater effect worsen as we inched down the main road.

'Are you excited for tomorrow?' Mum asked as we finally pulled off on to one of the quieter side roads.

'Definitely,' Will said, without hesitation. 'I'm going to eat a million vegan pigs in blankets.'

'They are nice. I need to peel some veg when we get in, to save time tomorrow . . .' Mum sighed. 'Christmas is all preparation when you're an adult. And I've always done it on my own.'

'Isn't Nick helping with the cooking prep this year?' I asked.

Mum gripped the steering wheel. 'No, he's busy. He's got to work.'

Will gave me a sneaky prod. 'On Christmas Eve?' he asked normally, innocently.

'Animals need looking after every day of the year, William,' Mum said, a little tersely.

'Well, yeah, but after he's tucked them in, he'll come over, right?' Will persisted. 'This morning he said he'd join our Christmas Eve movie night.'

'He's not going to be able to make it any more.' Mum pulled the car into the driveway.

Will opened his mouth again but Mum spoke before he could.

'Just leave it, Will.' Her face looked very tense in the rear-view mirror, like she was trying not to cry.

'Mum?' I asked, unbuckling myself and coming to pat her shoulder. 'Mum, are you and Nick . . . ?'

'We'll be alright,' she said, falsely cheery as she put her hand on top of mine. 'Nothing to worry about. Now, who wants a mince pie?' She let herself out the car.

Will gave me a look. 'That man had better be Santa, because if he's making Mum upset for no reason I'm going to put custard in his wellington boots.'

*

153

Mum peeled sprouts in the living room with the plastic bowl between her knees, as we all sat and watched quiz show Christmas specials on TV. The sleet outside had given way to a light powdery snow that didn't settle – it swirled about the pavement like tiny white marbles, skidding together in clumps.

Mum's phone went ping. She swiped it with her elbow, as her hands were wet. Her face lit up immediately. 'It's Nick,' she said. 'He's going to try to come over in a little bit after all.'

'That's nice,' I said, wondering how Nick was going to manage calling in to our house and getting to the North Pole all in one evening. Still, Mum seemed much cheerier after the text, and sang Christmas carols under her breath as she cut little crosses in the bottom of the sprouts.

Once the veggies were peeled, Mum and Will set about putting together the Christmas Eve tea. No one ever felt like a big meal after grazing constantly on nuts and chocolate all day, so our Christmas Eve tea was always a glorified picnic – little sandwiches shaped like trees, fruit, falafels, and hummus and carrot sticks to nibble on. We'd eat it on the floor of the living room whilst watching *The Muppet Christmas Carol*.

I glanced at the Christmas tree. Underneath were a few boxes of biscuits and chocolates Mum had received as gifts from people she worked with, as well as a few small presents between me, Mum and Will, like there were every year. A special present each for me and Will would always appear during the night from Father Christmas. But with Nick on his way over, I figured this year we might get them a little earlier.

The pathetic bits of snow coming down outside crackled against the window.

'What time is Nick coming?' Will asked, as the second Ghost made his appearance during the film.

'Oh, probably soon,' Mum said, checking her phone. 'He must be finishing up with the deer by now.'

Will bit noisily into a breadstick, his dislike of the situation coming through in the loud crunches. It made me wonder if I'd been ignoring the obvious all this time – if Nick really was an ordinary guy, and he and Mum were just going out, then he wouldn't really have a great excuse for being so late on Christmas Eve.

*And maybe*, I realised with a sinking feeling, *even after all the Santa-shaped mysteries and clues and theories, that's what was really going on.*

It was easier to believe Nick was Santa Claus than it was to admit that he was just a normal man who'd turned up at the most special time of year for our family of three. If he was Santa, then he wasn't some irresponsible guy who let his reindeer escape, because his reindeer could fly. If he was magical, then no wonder he was late sometimes; he was probably having to fix *lots* of kids'

156

broken toys, not only Will's. If he was Father Christmas, we could excuse him for being busy on Christmas Eve because he really would have other things to do. If he *wasn't* . . . well, then he was just letting my mum down.

I watched Mum check her phone as a text came in and felt a lurch in my stomach as her face fell with disappointment.

The magic of Christmas Eve felt spoiled, in a way that it never had before. Christmas had always been our time, just the three of us, and now . . .

. . . I wished we'd never even met Nick.

# Twenty

We all went to bed at the same time. Nick had never shown up.

Mum made a show of putting out a plate and a glass for Santa – a mince pie and sherry, as always – and then followed us up the stairs after turning the tree lights off.

I couldn't sleep.

I rolled about in bed, trying to switch my thoughts off, trying to drift into sleep, but it just wasn't happening. I checked my clock. It was gone ten o'clock: the last two hours of Christmas Eve.

There was a creak, and I looked up sharply as my bedroom door opened. For a second I thought a jolly fat man wearing red was going to walk in, but of course it was Will.

'Harps,' he whispered. 'You awake?'

'Obviously,' I whispered back, sitting up. 'Will, what are we going to *do*?'

He held up a torch. In his other hand was a tin of Heaven Custard. 'I'm getting revenge.'

'You're not serious.'

'I'm deadly serious. Look at my face – there's never been anyone more serious in the history of the universe.'

I sighed. 'If we get caught . . .'

'We won't. We'll be back home in half an hour, max. Come on, get dressed warmly. I'll meet you at the front door.' He slipped out.

Outside, the snow had started coming down properly, falling in thick clumps that stole the echo from the night air; it settled heavily on Will and me as we walked quickly down the street. It wasn't as scary as I'd thought it would be – streetlamps lit the way and there were cats prowling about trying to catch the snowflakes in their paws.

'It's cold,' I said from somewhere inside my coat. I was glad I'd worn my hat, scarf and gloves. 'Will, do you really think he's still going to be at the farm?'

'Even if he isn't, his wellies might be,' he said menacingly, brandishing the tin of custard.

It didn't take long to walk there, and all evidence of our route was covered by the quickly falling snow. Farmer Llama's didn't have a big security gate or anything like that – there was usually someone in a shed making sure everyone parked correctly, but at approaching midnight on Christmas Eve, the place was deserted.

Except for a big red pickup truck. One we recognised.

'He's here,' Will said, pulling his scarf down. 'I bet he's with the reindeer.'

Nerves had started fireworking in my stomach. We were going to be in *so much* trouble if we got caught. I followed Will down to the Staff Only door, watching nervously as he pushed it. It swung open, and no alarms started screaming, so he slipped through.

Of course I had to follow him.

The farm park felt weird at night. The horses and sheep were nowhere to be seen – no doubt safely tucked into their barns and shelters to keep warm – but the wallabies were hopping about in the snow, and the owls in the large aviary were swooping to and fro, their wide eyes glowing like lanterns in the moonlight.

We walked quickly towards the reindeer barn, following the light of Will's torch. I clung to his arm, too scared of the dark and the animal noises to walk by myself. He didn't shake me off, though, and walked steadily so we were stuck together in a half-hug for safety.

I didn't expect to see the reindeer out – it was night

after all, and Nick had told us how he tucked them in to sleep in the barn every night at ten on the dot, but to my surprise seven of them were trotting around the field as we approached, tossing their big heads and snorting as if they were in distress.

The mood for custard-related revenge evaporated.

'Something's wrong,' Will said.

We went towards the fence, and the reindeer came straight up to us. I could see that their plain red and jingle bell straps had been swapped out for leather and fur harnesses that looked extremely heavy-duty.

'Meteor?' I said, reading the name embroidered into the closest one. 'Nice to see you not on the roof . . .'

Meteor tossed her head, making me and Will step back, nervous about her antlers, but she meant us no harm. She made sure we were watching her and then trotted over to the closed barn door and knocked her antlers against it, hard

'She wants us to go in.' I grabbed Will's hand, my disappointment in Nick giving way to sharp concern. 'What if he's hurt? Or stuck?'

Will had gone pale. 'Where was that other door?'

We found it round the side, the No Entry sign surrounded by that beautiful wreath. Ignoring the sign, we pressed on the handle and pushed hard at the door until it creaked and scraped open. A wonderful straw smell came from inside, and we tumbled through the doorway into the large barn itself.

We caught ourselves and stood upright, our eyes taking in the sight in front of us.

Where there might have been farm equipment, a tractor or a combine harvester in a normal barn, stood a *sleigh*.

And not just any sleigh. This one was enormous. Easily the size of a lorry in length, and as tall and wide as a bus. The skis it rested on were gleaming silver steel, fastened to the thickest, heaviest looking branches of wood coming from the sleigh itself. The whole thing was stained a reddish brown, with evergreen pines and holly wrapped around the huge wooden bar at the front. Behind the bar was a bench-like seat, wide enough to seat four adults with room to spare. The loading area at the back was covered with a fur blanket that looked a lot like it was made of reindeer skin, and at the front were eight thick leather reins, all attached to nothing at all.

'Harper,' Will whispered, 'what does it feel like to be the cleverest person on Earth?'

'It feels pretty good,' I whispered back.

There was suddenly a clatter from the back of the sleigh, and we both jumped as a silhouette appeared. 'WHO'S THERE?' A booming voice echoed through the space.

There was a second where I was so scared I thought

I might scream, until Nick stepped into the light. His eyes went wide. 'H-Harper?' he spluttered. 'Will?'

I gave a little wave. Nick was wearing a suit of what looked like reindeer skin, dyed the same reddish brown as the sleigh, with white and grey trim around his buttons and cuffs. A heavy hat of the same colour was jammed down on his head. His hair was loose at the back and came around to meet his beard like a built-in scarf. He had huge black boots on his feet, which matched the big belt around his middle, thick like it was meant to support his back rather than just keep his coat closed.

'We were worried about you not showing up,' I said, deciding not to mention we'd initially been more custard-splatteringly mad than concerned.

Nick blinked in astonishment, then gave a huge sigh of relief. 'Well, thank goodness you're here,' he said. 'I need your help.'

# Twenty-One

'Help?' Will asked. 'What with?'

'Hold on a minute!' I yelled, holding my hands up to keep the two of them apart. 'You can't just carry on without discussing it!'

'It?' said Nick, though he was half-smiling and I was sure he knew what I meant.

'You're . . . you're Santa!' I said.

Nick smiled fully now, and shrugged. 'You're a smart kid, Harper. I thought you already knew.'

'Of course I already knew,' I said. 'But I wasn't sure if I *knew* I knew.'

Nick's dark eyes twinkled with that glittering magic I'd seen once or twice before, and this time it lingered. 'I'm sorry I didn't say anything. But you have to be careful about who you let know these things. I had to be sure.'

'You made the perfect Christmas cookies,' Will said in wonder. 'And the *really* good hot chocolates, the gingerbread castle, fixing my PuzzoCube—'

'The reindeer on the roof,' I added, grinning.

Nick looked embarrassed. 'That was my fault – I didn't remember to lock the barn door.'

'What about the snow?' Will frowned.

'Ah.' Nick's embarrassment continued. 'I was doing a test run, practising take-off at the house and we, er, didn't quite get high enough to avoid the snowy fall-out from the sleigh.'

'The presents you gave out at the dress rehearsal?' I asked.

'I was so in character, I just got carried away.'

'You knew exactly what was in the presents Mr Poltad had wrapped! And all the post!' I cried. 'Those were letters to Santa, weren't they? From all over the world, all the children writing to you?'

Nick nodded. He reached into his pocket and pulled out an envelope I recognised – so encrusted with glitter, sequins and glue that it was as stiff as a board. 'You really went to town with this one, Harper Hall.'

I stared at the envelope. 'You . . . got my letter.'

'I get all the letters,' he smiled. 'Ones covered in sequins, ones without stamps, ones burnt in the fireplace, ones sent through email . . . they all find me.'

'So you're like . . . magic?' Will blurted.

Nick blushed.

'And you're going out with our *mum*?'

'She's a very nice person,' Nick said, a bit helplessly. 'And right now, I wish she was here . . .' He glanced behind himself.

Me and Will went forwards to see. Round the back of the sleigh was an area for the reindeer to sleep, covered in straw and hay, and with food dishes attached to the metal bars. And in the stable area . . . was a reindeer. Lying down, and looking very sorry for herself.

'What's the matter with her?' I asked, going over. The reindeer's harness said 'Amor'.

'She won't walk,' Nick said. 'I can't see what's wrong with her.'

'You need a vet,' Will said. 'Why haven't you called Mum? She's been so upset you didn't come over. Why wouldn't you ask for her help?'

'I didn't want to worry her,' Nick said. 'And if she came here she'd have to leave you two alone on Christmas Eve. I couldn't have that, but I also couldn't risk you finding out about all this if she brought you along . . . though I suppose the reindeer is out of the barn on that secret now.'

Will stood up straight. 'You need her. It's gone eleven at night – aren't you late for delivering presents to Australia?'

Nick made a *pfft* noise. 'Christmas Eve doesn't work like that for me. There's more to this old thing than meets the eye.' He patted the sleigh affectionately. 'But I'm worried that Amor won't be able to pull tonight, and the sleigh needs a team of eight.'

'We need Mum,' I said. 'She'll be able to help Amor, I know she will!'

Nick brightened slightly, but then looked at his watch. 'She'll be asleep now. I can't call her. And I still need to harness the others—'

'I'll go,' Will said. 'I'll run home and get her.'

'Are you sure?'

'Sure as sure.' Will smiled.

Nick beamed back at him. Then frowned. 'William, why are you holding a tin of custard?'

'No reason,' Will said, hiding the tin behind his back. He winked at me, and I hid a smile behind my hand. 'Right. Wait here, I'm going to fetch Mum.' And he was out the door in a flash.

Nick and I looked at each other. It was extremely weird to be proven right about my theory. But even now he was in his full Santa get-up, Nick wasn't like the Santa from cartoons or cards – he was realer somehow. Not soft and jolly, but big and strong and rough, carved like the massive trees that had gone into making his sleigh, clad in skins and leather, and sturdy enough to command eight reindeer.

'Are you wearing reindeer skins?' I asked, wondering how Amor felt about that. 'You're not exactly what I expected,' I added.

'I never am,' he said kindly. 'It's not like the films. I dress for function, not style. Flying high and fast means you need a suit that's wind-and-snow-proof. Goggles, mittens, and fur.' He gave Amor the reindeer a stroke on the head, and she let out a low sound of affection. 'You couldn't do this job for long if you only concentrated on appearances. Now, Harper, I need your help here.' He went to the huge front gate of the barn and lifted it easily with one hand.

The snow outside whirled in, letting the cold in with it, and I saw that the seven other reindeer were stepping about anxiously in the field. They trotted forward when they spotted Nick, as if they were checking he was OK. He fussed them all, and now I was close I could see their names on their harnesses properly.

There was Sprinter, Starlet, Courser and Kit. And Meteor, Thunder, and Lightning. And Amor back in the barn, of course.

'What happened to Dasher, Dancer, Donner and Blitzen, from the song?' I asked.

Nick let out a short bark of a laugh. 'Legends last longer than reindeer,' he said apologetically. 'These are the great-great-something granddaughters of the ones from the song. There's never been a *Rudolph*, though,' he said, shaking his head. 'Someone made that up.'

'Can you fly the sleigh with seven reindeer?' I asked.

Nick pulled a doubtful face. 'For a short time, probably. All night? I don't think so. Still, maybe your mum can help Amor.' He took hold of a reindeer harness in each hand and steered the massive animals into the barn. 'Can you bring Meteor?' he called back at me.

Meteor gave me a look that said, *I'd like to see you try.*

I reached out and took hold of her harness. 'Please,' I said, 'I'll bring you some carrots?'

Meteor snorted, but started walking with me anyway.

'They don't actually like carrots,' Nick said, coming

back to get hold of Thunder and Lightning. 'They do like raisins as a treat, though.'

'I never knew that,' I said, helping Meteor to back into her space in front of the sleigh. She was a very good girl. 'What else do we have wrong?'

'Not everyone should feel compelled to leave me milk and cookies,' Nick said instantly, almost dragging the reindeer over to their reins. 'Or sherry and mince pies, for that matter. I'm a big guy who's driving all night . . . a pot of coffee and a sandwich would be a nice change sometimes.'

'I'll remember that,' I laughed.

There was a shout and I saw Will running back down the track, Mum hot on his heels, carrying her emergency vet bag.

# Twenty-Two

I couldn't imagine how this conversation was going to go.

*Mum, your boyfriend is Father Christmas. Try not to freak out?*

'It's Amor,' Nick said to Mum as she entered the barn and pulled her hat off.

'What's wrong with her?' Mum asked.

'She's lame,' Nick said, showing Mum over to the pen. 'She was fine this morning, Helen, but then she started to limp. I didn't want to trouble you, not on Christmas Eve.'

Mum clambered into the pen, tutting, and knelt beside Amor to check her over.

'I'm sorry,' Will said loudly, holding his hands up. 'But aren't you going to *say* anything, Mum? About the sleigh, the reindeer, the man in the red suit?'

'Oh, William,' she sighed, glancing at him. 'I'm not daft; I already knew, of course.'

'WHAT?' I yelped.

'How long have you known?' Will demanded as Nick started to laugh.

'Since just after we met, last year,' she said, rummaging in her bag.

'And you didn't tell us?' I couldn't believe this.

She gave Amor an injection. 'Think about it – would you have believed me? You would have thought I'd lost my marbles if I told you I was going to introduce you to my new boyfriend, Santa. And besides, Father Christmas' identity is the biggest secret in the world. We decided to tell you when you'd got to know him a bit better.' She stroked Amor. 'Her leg's inflamed. Looks like she might have stumbled into a rabbit-hole and hurt herself. She'll be alright, but no flying tonight.'

'That might be a problem . . .' Nick scratched at his beard. 'We're down to a team of seven.'

'Sorry, but that's doctor's orders.' She climbed out of the pen and folded her arms. 'And I'm not too happy with you, either.'

To my surprise, Nick blushed bright red and looked extremely contrite. 'It's just . . . my job is . . .'

'I know it's important,' Mum said. She walked over to Nick and touched him on the arm. 'I struggle to balance everything too – I send the kids to Breakfast Club and after school clubs so I can do the job I love; a job that keeps a roof over our heads. But I keep my promises to the kids and make time for them. They're just as important. *I'm* just as important. I know that on this night of the year especially your job is going to keep you busy, and that's OK. The problem is that you said you would be there, and you weren't.'

Nick raised his head and looked her in the eyes. 'I know. I *wanted* to be there tonight and I thought I'd be able to fit it all in. This is . . . new for me.'

'We all make mistakes,' Mum said with a smile. 'We can learn together. As a family.'

'As a family,' Nick agreed, taking both her hands in one of his. 'I'm sorry for not being there for you.'

'I forgive you.'

They smiled at each other and went in for a kiss.

Will started making throwing-up noises, and I covered my face with my gloved hands. There was no *way* I was going to look at *that*.

\*

Mum watched the reindeer drag the sleigh out of the barn with a concerned frown on her face. 'That empty harness looks wrong,' she said.

'I know, but you said yourself, there's no way Amor can fly.' Nick looked extremely worried. 'We'll just have to see how we get on without her. Maybe if we stay below cruising height, take-off won't be too much of a problem. We'll be at risk of being spotted by aeroplanes, though . . . I'll have to make some adjustments for that . . .' He trailed off, not sounding convinced by his own words.

I looked up, suddenly having an idea. 'Hey, does it have to be a *reindeer* pulling the sleigh?'

Everyone looked at me. 'What do you mean?' Mum asked.

'Well, we're on a farm,' I pointed out. 'Could you make another animal fly, and use them to pull the sleigh?'

'Technically, yes,' Nick said. 'But horses don't like heights, and cows don't fit the harness.'

I smiled. 'I wasn't thinking of a horse . . .'

Five minutes later, Mum was walking up the path leading behind her a very bewildered-looking llama.

'Is it honestly going to fly?' Will asked, as Mum steered it towards the sleigh.

181

'It'll have to,' I said. 'Nick needs to get going as soon as he can.'

Nick and Mum buckled the llama into one of the front two harnesses, the animal looking about at the reindeer, all of whom were wearing extremely unimpressed expressions.

'Perfect!' Mum stepped back to admire their handiwork.

Nick shook his head, but he was smiling. 'Well, it's worth a try.'

The sleigh was packed up, the reindeer and the llama were harnessed, and Nick was finally ready to set off into the night. The long paddock made a perfect runway for the sleigh, and the seven coursers were snorting and tossing their heads and ready to be off. The llama was looking extremely lost.

Mum was standing with her arms wrapped around herself, looking nervous. 'Be safe, won't you?' she said to Nick.

'I always am,' he promised. Then he looked at me and Will, who were standing to one side. Nick glanced at Mum, and she smirked. 'Are you two ready?' he asked.

'Ready?' Will repeated.

'For take-off.'

'We . . . we're coming with you?' I gasped.

'If you want to?' Nick patted the long bench-like seat at the front of the sleigh.

'Obviously!' Will launched himself on to the seat.

I looked back at Mum. 'Aren't you coming?'

'No thanks,' she said. 'I'm going to stay and look after Amor. But have fun! And hold on tight!'

My heart bursting with excitement, I clambered on to the sleigh beside Will. Nick squeezed in after me, taking up half the bench by himself. He snapped the reins, and the reindeer and llama suddenly stood to attention, heads pointing forward, looking out at the snow-covered field where they had to run.

I braced myself, ready to hear those cries of *On Sprinter! On Starlet! On Thunder and Lightning!* but they didn't come. Instead, Nick gave a roar that seemed to be in a song-like language, and the animals began to charge. Their hooves dug into the grass of the paddock, and they charged forwards, and then *upwards*, their legs ploughing up through the sky as though they were running up an invisible hill. Even the llama was flying just like the others, its land-bound life apparently forgotten.

The sleigh tipped back sharply, and I tried not to scream as we were all thrown backwards against the massive cargo hold behind us.

'Hold on tight!' Nick bellowed as the sleigh soared into the sky. The reindeer seemed to find some sort of magical strength, and their legs moved faster than ever. And suddenly we were so high up that the farm below looked like a toy playset, and the houses around were tiny little boxes.

My fright giving way to excitement, I leaned around Will to look at the fairyland of lights below, at the swirls of snow that were covering the windows and pavements under a white blanket. The air in the sky was ice-cold and made me want to cough, but it felt like breathing starlight and magic, and after a moment the cold didn't seem to matter so much. At cruising height, the reindeer levelled off, and their charge through the dark slowed just enough for Will and me to look at each other and burst out laughing.

'This is unreal,' he said.

'It's magic,' I replied.

And beside me, Nick gave a soft chuckle, and snapped the reins once more to drive the reindeer on through the night.

# Twenty-Three

We flew on, past stars and lights and confused owls that screeched as we shot past. The reindeer didn't tire, the llama kept pace as if it had been doing this all its life, and Nick kept his goggles over his eyes and his hands on the reins as he directed the coursers on some invisible road.

Snow battered at us, not getting a chance to settle as we were travelling too fast. Me and Will gripped the bar of the sleigh hard in our gloved hands, the wind stinging our cheeks when we dared to lift our heads out of the safety of our scarves

After a few minutes, Nick pulled the reins to turn the reindeer around to the right. 'Hang on, you two, we're going to make a landing shortly, and the girls don't take it slowly.'

The reindeer banked hard and began to descend almost straight down; it was like being on a rollercoaster. I had to brace my legs against the curved front of the sleigh to stop myself falling out altogether, and Will had his eyes shut tight as he held on to the safety bar.

Through the dark, lights sprung back into sight as the streets came towards us, every fairy light and glowing street-lamp brightening as we approached. The peaked rooftops of the houses below were now visible, and I could see every tile. For a second I wondered if we were going to crash because we were still going so fast!

But I didn't need to worry – the reindeer clearly knew what they were doing. They gently slowed their magical charge through the night air until it was just a trot, and then they pulled up on the top of a row of terraced houses that was long enough to take the enormous sleigh and all seven of the reindeer plus a bonus llama.

'Where are we?' I asked, looking around at the silent street. I didn't recognise any of the buildings, which were all made of pale creamy stone. There was a large village square close by, with a small river running alongside it.

'This is Little Wyverns,' Nick said. 'Small village in Nottinghamshire. You two stay where you are. The rooftops can be dangerous if you don't know what you're doing.'

'Are you going to deliver presents?' Will asked, turning around in his seat.

'I certainly am. Now, this is where the magic really takes hold.' Nick went around to the back of the sleigh, out of sight. I felt, rather than saw, the movement of the great big reindeer-skin cover that was roped over the cargo hold, and then Nick came back around to us, two sacks over his massive shoulders. They looked old, those sacks, but tough and big enough for me to have climbed inside and had room to spare.

'I won't be long,' Nick said, with a wink, and he started to walk away.

'Wait!' I called. 'These houses don't have chimneys – what are you going to do?'

'Chimneys?' Nick snorted. 'As if I'm going to fit down a *chimney*.' And with another step, he seemed to drop straight through the roof of the house, without so much as breaking a single splinter, sinking as though the tiles were water, vanishing out of sight.

'So he can walk through walls,' Will said, after a second of stunned silence. 'Of course he can.'

'Can you believe this?' I squirmed in delight in the sleigh, watching the reindeer fidget as they waited for their master to come back. 'This is *real*, Will!'

'I know,' he said, eyes full of the starry sky. 'I never imagined anything like this.'

We weren't kept waiting long. Less than ten minutes after he left, Nick reappeared at the side of the sleigh, sacks empty and looking very pleased with himself.

'That was so fast!' I cried.

'It's Christmas Eve,' he said, 'and I'm Father Christmas. Time works differently around me. Tonight, the air is full of magic. I can make llamas fly, and bend and twist time as I need to. And I *do* need to, in order to get all the way around the world in one night.' He fastened the reindeer-skin covering back over the cargo hold and got settled beside me again, adjusting his goggles and mittens before picking up the reins.

The reindeer took off once more, their hooves digging into the dark of the night like it was something solid, but this time they didn't shoot as high into the icy sky. They flew just below the clouds, the snow falling thickly around us. We were low enough now to be able to make out where we were going.

Though it was the middle of the night, because it was Christmas there were plenty of lights still on. I could see rainbow glows from inside the houses and flats, shifting from red to green to yellow as the fairy lights went through their colour-changing cycle, keeping the sleeping houses company overnight.

The snow continued to fall, coating everything like icing on a gingerbread house. It turned orange-brown bricks cream, and black Tarmac roads into grey granite like mountainsides.

'It feels like we could be the only people in the world,' Will said, looking down at the empty roads where not a single car or bicycle disturbed the white below.

'I'm glad we're not,' I said. I glanced up at Nick, who was concentrating on driving. Had he meant it, what he'd said to Mum? Was he going to try to make time for family? For *our* family?

Was Nick a permanent addition to the Hall family now?

I found that I didn't hate the idea. Actually, I rather liked it. I'd never been sure about the idea of having a stepdad, but if it was one who listened, was kind, cared for animals and made Mum happy . . . I could accept that. And if he *was* Father Christmas? Well, that was just a bonus.

As if reading my thoughts, Nick tapped my arm. 'I'm sorry about before,' he shouted over the rush of the wind. 'About nearly missing the play, and not making it for dinner. Your mum's right – I do need to make time for family.'

'For our family?' I asked.

He looked at me, and gave a firm nod. 'For our family,' he said.

# Twenty-Four

The night glittered with stars, lights and magic. We raced through the air, three humans pulled by seven enchanted reindeer and one emergency llama. Their hooves dug into the air as though there was a road only they could see, and the snow streamed out behind the enormous sleigh like a vapour trail, leaving a milky sheen behind it.

Nick parked the sleigh on rooftops that could handle its size (plus the animals) and Will and I helped pass him the great sacks of toys from under the reindeer-skin tarpaulin. Nick lifted each sack as if it weighed nothing, stepping through walls and chimney-stacks to get inside the houses and leave presents for all the sleeping children.

The night seemed to go on forever. The darkness never lifted, the stars glittered as brightly as ever and the snow kept on coming like it would never end.

Even with Nick's magic stretching time like elastic, it didn't work the same way on ordinary people like me and Will, and after a while we found ourselves yawning and our eyes doing very long, slow blinks. Despite all the excitement, I found myself thinking about going home to my warm bed, and sleeping until the wonder of Christmas Day arrived.

Nick noticed us yawning. 'Ready for home?' he called.

I wanted to say no. It had been the most magical night of my life, and I didn't want it to end. But I was so tired I was worried about falling out of the sleigh. 'I think so.'

'It's been amazing,' Will added sleepily.

Nick smiled through a beard full of snow. 'Home, then.' He snapped the reins and the coursers charged right – the llama giving a bleat of surprise – tilting the sleigh as we banked hard, heading back the way we came.

*

Mum was standing in the paddock as we descended. She waved as she saw us barrelling through the snow, then hopped safely on to a fence as the enormous sleigh landed on the ground. We skidded to a halt just ahead of the barn.

'You look frozen!' she gasped, helping me and Will down from the sleigh. Now we'd stopped racing through the sky, the cold seemed to have taken hold properly and I was starting to shiver.

Nick jumped down and went around the back of the sleigh as Will shook his hat free of snow and tried to explain what it had been like.

'In the sky! Flying!' He made zooming motions with his hand.

Mum laughed. 'You're exhausted. But I'm so glad you had fun.'

Nick came around from the cargo area, holding another huge sack. 'Just one small thing, before you go home,' he said.

My heart leapt. 'Presents! For us!'

Nick held up a finger. 'Not just a present. A wish.'

'A wish?' I blinked.

'Letters you send to me are wishes,' he said. 'Not all of them come true, but I do my best. And since you helped me tonight, you can have a bonus wish here and now. What is it you want?' He put the sack down. 'Make a wish, Harper, Will.'

My mind raced. I thought about asking for money, jewels, a flying llama, tickets to go to a Rainbow Catz concert. But then I thought about Mum. Mum, who tried every single Christmas to make things magical for me and Will, all by herself. Working long hours with animals that barked and scratched and pooped on the examination table, never taking a real break.

I went over to Nick. 'I have a wish,' I said, 'but I have to whisper it.'

'That's alright.' He pulled his hat off to hear properly, his long white hair buffeted by the cold air.

And I whispered my wish.

He smiled. 'Consider it done, Harper. What about you, Will?'

'I can't think of anything,' he shrugged.

'What about Henry?' I suggested. 'Wouldn't you like to be best mates again?'

He sighed and, to my surprise, shook his head. 'Yeah, I would,' he said. 'But I don't want to wish for that to happen. I want him to be my friend again because he wants to be, not because magic made it happen.'

'Very wise, Will,' Mum said, giving him a sideways hug. 'But how about . . .' and she said something softly to him.

He laughed. 'Yeah, alright. I wish for a vintage collector's set of PuzzoCube cards.' He grinned roguishly.

Nick gave him a bemused look, and started rummaging in his sack. He searched for a good long minute until he brought out a gift-wrapped package and held it out to Will. 'Don't open it until morning.'

'I won't.' Will took the package and smiled. 'Thanks . . . Nick. Father Christmas.'

'Stepfather Christmas,' I said, suddenly realising. And everyone laughed.

'Come on, you two,' Mum said. 'Nick has a job to do.'

'I certainly do. Thank you, all of you, for your help tonight.' Nick shook Will's hand and mine, and planted a kiss on Mum's cheek. Then he clapped his hands, and the reindeer, expertly trained along with the llama which seemed to be enjoying itself, began to turn the sleigh around in the field to face the right way for a take-off.

'You will be over for Christmas dinner, won't you?' I asked Nick.

'I promise,' he said. 'I'm going to do my best to make time for work *and* family.' He gave Mum a smile and she returned it. 'I'll see you all tomorrow.'

We stepped back, out of the way as the sleigh was readied for the next part of its journey. Nick clambered into the seat and took up the reins. His deep red suit was brilliant against the snow, and the evergreens wrapped around the carved wood of the sleigh were glittering with ice and frost. He adjusted his flight goggles and gloves, and gave us a wave.

We waved back frantically as the coursers began to charge again, climbing up through the darkness, the sleigh dragged up into the sky behind them, onwards towards their next destination.

# Christmas Day

Christmas is still Christmas, even if your sort-of stepdad is Santa Claus. That meant opening presents whilst still in our pyjamas, eating chocolate oranges for breakfast, and the whole house smelling deliciously of gingerbread, stuffing, roast potato seasoning and herbs before noon.

'How unexpected!' Will said, as he unwrapped his 1970s PuzzoCube cards. 'Just what I wished for.'

'What did you wish for, Harps?' Mum asked me as I unwrapped a box set of the *Murder at The Tea-Party* novels I was constantly borrowing from the library.

'This was what I asked for in my letter.' I showed her the books. 'He really did read it.'

'What about your bonus wish from last night?' she asked, looking under the tree and seeing there wasn't anything left to unwrap. 'You whispered another wish to Nick, didn't you? What was that?'

'You'll see,' I said mysteriously. Because the thing I'd wished for couldn't be wrapped, and therefore wasn't under the tree at all.

I was slightly worried about Nick keeping his promise about coming for dinner, but my worries quickly evaporated when he arrived just after noon, arms full of presents and with a homemade Christmas cake.

'Thanks so much,' Will called from the kitchen table, where he was already working on his new puzzles.

'And for everything,' I added from the sofa, already halfway through the second *Murder at The Tea-Party* book.

'You're very welcome,' Nick boomed, putting his things down. 'What can I do to help?'

Mum soon had him making vegan custard and dream topping, as she bustled about ensuring the nut roast didn't burn whilst stirring gravy on the hob with one hand. Christmas dinner always seemed to take ages and then be ready all of a sudden, but me and Will were used to that, and we flung ourselves into our places at the table just in time for Nick and Mum to carry everything through.

There were crackers Nick had brought with him, which went off like cannons and had glittering sparks fly from the burst-open ends, as well as gifts like miniature binoculars and rolls of biscuits inside. The food was delicious: the right combination of Mum's experimentation and Nick's clearly expert cooking, and by the time the plates were cleared, everyone was sleepy and happy and ready to sit down in front of a film we'd seen before until we'd digested enough to make room for the cake Nick had made.

We'd just sat on the sofa, when the doorbell rang.

'I'll get it,' Will said, heaving himself upright. He went out of the room, and I listened hard to the sound of him answering the door.

'Oh, Henry,' I heard him say in surprise.

Mine and Mum's eyes met, and I crept out of the living room to spy properly. I could see Henry standing on the doorstep, holding a wrapped present and looking a bit sheepish.

'Hey, Will,' he said. 'Um. Happy Christmas.' He held the present out.

'Thanks . . . I didn't get you anything though,' Will said.

'That's OK, I just wanted to say sorry. For before. For thinking things had to be different between us.'

'It's OK,' Will said, and he took a deep breath. 'Just because you don't want to be my boyfriend doesn't mean we have to stop being friend-friends.'

Henry gave a small laugh. 'I know. I was being an idiot. Guess being banged on the head in the road finally knocked some sense into me.'

'About time something did. Hey – did you see I'd got *Dracula Death Mansion 2*?' Will asked.

'What – really?'

'Yeah, you want a go on it?'

'Yeah!'

The door closed as Will let Henry in. 'Mum, Henry's here,' he yelled before the two of them thundered upstairs to Will's bedroom and their precious game.

I went back into the living room. 'I guess they're friends again now.'

'I knew they would be,' Mum said. 'I'm very proud of Will. Of both of you,' she added. Then she frowned, and looked from me to Nick and back again. 'Are either of you going to tell me what that wish was?'

I looked at Nick, trying to hide the smile that was fighting its way up my face. 'Um . . . Nick, did you want to say?'

'I will do,' he said. He turned to Mum. 'Helen,' he said seriously, 'you're always doing things for other people, so Harper and I think it's time you had a little time to yourself, and did something you've always wanted to do.'

'What's this?' Mum said. 'What do you mean?'

'I mean . . . I want you to come with me, to my other house. Up in Finland.' Nick smiled through his beard. 'Come and stay with me for a while, all three of you, to see the Northern Lights.'

Mum gave a weird sort of squeaky gasp, her hands flying to her mouth. 'I've aways wanted to see . . . But when?'

'Tonight!'

'Tonight?' Mum's hands dropped again. 'But it's Christmas Day, how will we get to the airport, how can we—'

'Oh, we're not flying on a plane,' I said, starting to laugh. 'But you will definitely need to wrap up warm.'

'Amor's leg is much better already, so the ride should be nice and smooth,' Nick added.

Mum's eyes were as wide as dinner plates. 'You planned this, Harper?'

'It was my wish,' I said. 'Happy Christmas, Mum.'

'Oh!' Mum swept me up into a hug and squeezed me so hard I thought my Christmas dinner might reappear. 'I don't know what to say.'

'Never mind talking,' I said, 'we need to pack! We'll set off tonight and have Christmas in the Arctic, with the penguins!'

'There aren't penguins in the Arctic,' Mum said, remembering.

'Maybe we can take a detour via the South Pole,' Nick mused, stroking his beard. 'There are a few weeks before schools starts again, aren't there?'

We laughed, gathering ourselves together in our newly expanded family. And I marvelled at how easily we'd made room for a new person, how families were spaces that expanded, with more love each time.

Outside, kids raced up and down the snowy pavements on new bikes or kicked footballs or built snowpeople in regiments along the road. The sky was a clear blue, the air was crisp, and the world felt full of magic, and possibility.

# Acknowledgements

Huge thanks must go to my editor, Lena McCauley, for asking to hear this story in the first place, and for finding it a home. I hope my initial pitch of *what if you really did see Mummy kissing Santa Claus?* has lived up to the hype!

Thanks also to my wonderful publicist and marketing teams, particularly to Dom, Beth and Katie for all the festive cheer – and biscuits! – along the way. Sorry not sorry for dressing up as an elf on the video call that time . . . Thank you to Ruth, Matt and Adele for neatening up my work and telling me where commas are supposed to go. And shoutout to designer Sam and illustrator Nicolas for the wonderful cover that makes me feel incredibly festive every time I see it!

Thank you to Claire Wilson, a true gift of an agent, for going along with another left-field idea of mine, and for all the encouragement – may you always get everything you wish for.

And to Anton and Joseph, for putting up with me blasting a Christmas playlist in March, singing carols during a heatwave and not batting an eyelid when I started wearing a Santa hat on weekdays . . . thank you, I love you.

# About the Author

L. D. Lapinski lives just outside Sherwood Forest with their family, a lot of books, and a cat called Hector. They are the author of *The Strangeworlds Travel Agency* series, and the standalone *Jamie*.

When they aren't writing, L. D. can be found cosplaying, drinking a lot of cherry cola, and taking care of a forest of succulent plants. L. D. first wrote a book aged seven; it was made of lined paper and Sellotape, and it was about a frog who owned an aeroplane. When L. D. grows up, they want to be a free-range guinea pig farmer.

You can find them on social media @ldlapinski or at ldlapinski.com

# Want more from L. D. Lapinski?

Look out for *Stepfather Christmas 2*,
coming in time for Christmas 2024,
but in the meantime you can
try these incredible books!

A joyful story of bravery, acceptance and finding your place in the world.

# AT THE

# STRANGEWORLDS

## · TRAVEL AGENCY ·

**EACH SUITCASE TRANSPORTS YOU TO
A DIFFERENT WORLD. ALL YOU HAVE
TO DO IS STEP INSIDE . . .**